the secrets we hide

USA TODAY & *WALL STREET JOURNAL* BESTSELLING AUTHOR

BECCA STEELE

THE SECRETS WE HIDE

THE FOUR - BOOK 2

BECCA STEELE

The Secrets We Hide (The Four, #2)

Editing by One Love Editing

Becca Steele

www.authorbeccasteele.com

AUTHOR'S NOTE

The author is British, and British English spellings and phrases are used throughout.

To my siblings.
This one's for you.
(Sorry not sorry I forced you to read my books.)

That was how dishonesty and betrayal started, not in big lies but in small secrets.

— AMY TAN, *THE BONESETTER'S DAUGHTER*

1

caiden

Cassius navigated through the street, barely any wider than the width of his SUV. His eyes narrowed in concentration, the high stone walls on either side bearing down on us. I grasped my phone so tightly I thought it would shatter in my grip, reading the message over and over.

Snowflake: It might not be Arlo Davis. I think it could be ARGO NAVIS. A boat at the docks. I'm going there to check it out now. Will let you know what I find.

Fear for Winter's safety mixed with the anger and betrayal already coursing through me, fizzing through my veins.

Concentrating on my anger was easiest right now.

I'd never let anyone get close enough to have the power to hurt me, not after Christine Clifford had fucked up my world, tearing my family apart. Winter had somehow managed to get through my defences, and it fucking *hurt* that she'd done this to me. I couldn't bring myself to watch the video again, but it was burned into my mind, Granville's lips on my girl's...

Fuck. I lashed out, punching the back of the seat in front of me, Weston jerking forwards in his seat as my fist connected with the leather.

"What the fuck, Cade?" he shouted, turning to glare at me. He took in my face and his eyes widened, and he turned around without another word. Guess I looked as bad as I felt.

"I can't track her phone," he muttered to Cassius, his finger scrolling through the app we all had that allowed us to locate each other. "Something must've happened to it."

My stomach tightened, and my throat clenched.

"Mate, show me the video." Zayde leaned over to me, speaking in a low voice, holding his hand out. I opened the message thread and handed him my phone wordlessly, then slumped back, closing my eyes.

Silence.

"I don't think you should jump to conclusions," he said finally, handing my phone back. "Yeah, it looks incriminating as fuck, but..." His voice trailed off, defeated. "Shit. I can't lie. Mate, I'd be fucking livid if that was my girl."

"Yeah." I threw my phone onto the seat between us. "Hard to ignore the evidence when it's right in front of you."

He tapped the screen. "You've got a voicemail."

I hadn't noticed, with all the other shit that was going on. I retrieved my phone from where I'd thrown it, dragging my thumb across it to unlock the screen. There was a text from her, too. I'd ignored it when I was reading her latest message, but now I took it in.

Snowflake: We need to talk. NOTHING HAPPENED. Check your voicemail. Phone me as soon as you get this, PLEASE.

I dialled my inbox.

"Cade, it's me. Well, I guess you already know that. That video isn't how it looks." Her voice cracked, and it fucking *hurt*. "James cornered me in the library, and he had a black eye. What you saw in the video was me showing concern and trying to comfort him, and then—" I heard a muffled cry. "—and then, he tried to kiss me, and I froze. As soon as I realised what was going on, I stamped on his foot as hard as I could to make him stop. Cade, you have to believe me...I would never...I only want you."

I threw the phone. Hearing her that upset killed me, but the way she'd looked at him on the video, like she cared... They had history. They'd fucked. Before me. Before she was mine.

I didn't know when I'd started thinking of her as mine, rather than a girl I liked to fuck, but it happened, and now she was in my head. Fucking with me.

Blinding jealousy raged through my body, and I clenched my fists, gritting my teeth, attempting rationality. I needed to step back, to calm the fuck down, but there was no being rational when it came to her.

"Mate." Zayde looked over at me, concern flashing in his eyes. So unusual for him to show any emotion, it took me aback. He reached down and swiped my phone from where it landed on the floor. "Mind if I listen to the voicemail?"

I shook my head.

He adopted his usual blank expression as he listened to the message, then turned to me. "Maybe she's putting on an act, but she sounds genuine to me."

"Why didn't she tell me, though? Why wait?"

"You need to talk."

Yeah.

I locked the anger and hurt away and switched my focus to the immediate situation—finding Winter and getting her away from any danger. The only thing that mattered, right now, was her safety. Fuck, I'd rather she ended up with Granville than in danger or hurt. I was furious with her for being so reckless, but at the same time, I understood. If I'd been in her situation? I'd have done exactly the same.

Finally away from Alstone town and out on the open road, Cass put his foot down, increasing our speed, navigating with one hand on the wheel, the other clenched tightly around the gearstick. The atmosphere in the car was thick with tension, only slightly easing up once we were flying down the familiar coastal road, the ocean on our left, past Alstone Castle, towards the docks.

As we drew closer, Cassius slowed down, the SUV's headlights cutting through the darkness. The only light came from the stars that occasionally appeared between the clouds that covered the night sky.

"Cass!" my brother hissed urgently. "Stop!"

My eyes followed the direction of his outstretched arm, his finger jabbing against the windscreen.

Winter's car.

Tucked away, off the side of the road, the matte-black paint blending into the shadows.

Cassius pulled to a stop just behind the Fiat 500, sending a shower of dust and gravel flying up around the wheels, and I jumped out, not bothering to wait for him to turn the engine off. Jogging over to the front of her car, I placed my hand on the smooth metal surface.

It was ice-cold.

Fuck.

I jogged back to the SUV, leaning into Weston's open window. "The engine's stone cold. She must've been here a while, and the fact she hasn't come back—" I cut my words off abruptly, scrubbing my hand across my face, unable to articulate my worst fears.

"Shit," Cass swore softly, his eyes darkened with worry. "I'll park here. Eyes and ears open, all of you. Let's go get our girl."

2

caiden

I shrugged off my suit jacket, rolling up my shirtsleeves, ignoring the biting cold air. Tugging at my collar, I wished I'd been wearing my usual jeans and hoodie. Don't get me wrong; I liked a sharp suit, tailored to fit, but I was always more comfortable dressed down. Right now? This suit was a fucking inconvenience.

"Here," Cass grunted, emerging from the boot and throwing me a bundle of fabric. I opened it to find a black hoodie, and I pulled it on over my shirt, tugging the hood over my head.

"Cheers, mate."

He nodded and tipped his head towards the road leading to the docks, his brows raised in a question.

"Let's go."

We all filed into a line, working together as we'd always done, seamlessly, silently, reading each other's minds. When we reached the entrance to the docks, I held up a hand behind my back, signalling for them to wait.

Peering around the corner, my eyes scanned the area, cataloguing every detail.

The white painted guard hut by the entrance barrier was empty, and the whole place seemed quiet. Too quiet.

I noted the cameras mounted on high stalks and on the side of the guard hut, and indicated to my boys so they were aware. Crossing the entrance, I flattened my body against the side of the hut, Z in position next to me, poised and ready.

"Nothing. Except...that full mug of coffee."

I followed Zayde's gaze, noting an Alstone Holdings branded ceramic mug, balanced on the table in front of the monitors, and a dog-eared open book next to it, face down. The spine was creased, the title and author name written in a language I couldn't read.

"Stay alert. Someone must've been here. Recently," I told the others in a low voice.

"The coffee looks cold to me," Cassius commented, peering through the window. "There's a film on the top."

Fuck. Whoever had been on guard duty could be long gone.

Time to check out the rest of the docks.

We moved stealthily around the corner of a low building, avoiding the cameras. Where was Winter?

My gaze was drawn to a crumbling stone building by the water's edge, set apart from the rest of the docks. Every single instinct in me screamed that this was where I needed to be.

Keeping to the shadows, I ran.

I burst through the doorway, the door itself wide open, hanging at an angle.

Fuck. I couldn't see anything.

I heard the sounds of my boys falling in behind me, a solid presence at my back. I straightened up.

Whatever was going on here, we'd get to the bottom of it. No one fucked with what was ours and got away with it.

We'd bury them.

Lights flickered on overhead, and I spun around to see Cass looking over at me, his hand poised over a light switch to the left of the doorway.

Zayde, Cassius, and Weston came to stand next to me, and we took in the square space we were standing in, with a long corridor off to the left. Distinct footprints and marks were visible on the dusty wooden floorboards, a clear indication someone had been that way recently.

Zayde glanced down the corridor, then back to the door, then pulled out his phone, dialling a number.

"I need a favour... Yeah. Backup... Not sure what we're dealing with. Sending the address now... Yeah."

He stabbed the phone to end the call and slipped it into his pocket. "Cade, check this out with Cass. Be careful. Me and West will go to the gate to wait for the others, and West can check the security feeds in the guard hut."

"Sure." I barely heard him as he threw the words over his shoulder and disappeared with Weston.

"Follow me." I took command of the situation, skulking down the dimly lit corridor, the floorboards creaking underfoot. The corridor seemed endless. As we moved along, hugging the wall, a door came into view, gunmetal grey, studs around the edge, solid and impenetrable.

I sped up, focused on that door.

The glint of something shiny caught my eye, and I stopped, crouching down to get a better look, careful not to disturb anything. Scanning the floor, I squinted into the corner where the stone wall met the ground. I stretched out, and my hand closed around a small oblong object. Pulling it into the light, I flipped it over.

Winter's phone.

Shit.

"That explains why we couldn't track her," I muttered under my breath as I traced my finger over the cracked screen, the phone completely unresponsive as I attempted to power it on.

Clambering to my feet and pocketing the phone, I stared at Cassius, trying to stop the fucking panic that was trying to rise up inside me. This was why I didn't get close to people. After my mum died, I swore I wouldn't let any woman have that power over me. Not for the first time, I asked myself how Winter had managed to slip through my defences.

I shook my head, straightening up, ignoring Cass' curious look. These thoughts had no place here. All that mattered was finding her. Everything else could wait.

"Let's check this door, yeah? We need to find Winter."

Cassius nodded, all business, slipping around me and moving forwards a few paces until he was in front of the door. "You ready?"

I joined him, keeping to the side, all my senses on high alert. "Ready."

He grabbed the door handle and pushed.

The door opened, to the surprise of both of us, especially considering there was a number panel to the side of the door, clearly there to unlock the entry to the room. We exchanged glances; then I nodded to Cassius, and he pushed the door all the way open, his muscles straining with the effort as he threw his weight against the thick, heavy metal.

The room was dark, and Cass and I both turned on the flashlights on our phones, illuminating the space.

It was completely empty.

Fuck.

There was nothing to give us any clues about what it was used for. Dirty, damp stone walls and floors, boarded-up windows, and old, rusting iron rings cemented into the stones, probably there since the place was built.

"Where's Winter?" Distress bled through Cassius' voice, and my stomach turned. Where was she?

Had she been taken somewhere?

The thought sent bile rising in my throat.

"Winter!" My shout bounced off the walls, echoing around us.

"Keep it down, will ya?" Cassius hissed. "We don't know if anyone else is around. Whoever was in the guard hut had to have gone somewhere."

He was right. We had to proceed with caution.

"Alright, mate. We need to check out the rest of the area. She was here—we've got her phone as proof."

"C'mon. Z called for backup, didn't he? We should wait for them to get here; we don't know who or what else might be here. The last thing we need to do is get into a dodgy situation."

I nodded, stalking out of the room, back down the corridor, and out into the cool night air to wait for Zayde's contacts to turn up, Cassius right beside me.

We crossed the docks and reached the entrance, where Zayde and Weston waited, just as a blacked-out, nondescript van pulled up, a guy with a balaclava obscuring his face in the driver's seat.

"Z. Show us where to go."

Zayde looked between us. "Keep a lookout. We'll do a sweep of the area. Catch up with you after." I nodded at him, and he swung himself into the van.

I turned to my brother. "Did you sort the security footage?"

"Yeah, sorted. Fucking camera on the gate was on the blink, and the ones in the docks were facing the wrong way. All seems too convenient, if you ask me."

What the fuck was going on in this place?

When Zayde returned to us, the van speeding away, he motioned with his head towards the road, and we jogged towards Cassius' SUV.

"What are we gonna do about Winter's car?" Cass paused by his open door.

"Already thought of that. I'll take care of it." Weston dug around in his pockets and held up his key ring, grinning triumphantly. "Still got her spare car key. I never gave it back after the respray. I'll follow you back."

"Meet ya back at the house." Cass swung up into the driver's seat, and I jogged around to the other side. Zayde slid into the back, while Weston got into Winter's tiny car. I smirked, the worry temporarily pushed from my mind as I watched him try to adjust the cramped seat to fit his large frame.

"Hold on," Cass muttered and threw the car into a U-turn, the tyres screeching in protest. He shot down the empty road, Weston following behind, keeping up as best as he could in Winter's car.

"Anything?" I already knew the answer before I even asked Zayde the question.

"Sorry, mate. No sign of her, or of whoever was on duty. Only place we didn't look was the building you and Cass already checked."

"Yeah, she was long gone from there." Cassius' voice was sombre. "Where is she?"

"My boys will keep an eye on the docks. But...fuck," Zayde muttered. "We need to find her."

Yeah. We did.

Before it was too late.

3

winter

I*t's so dark.*

Slowly, carefully, I blinked my eyes open, becoming aware of an intense, throbbing pain in my head. I groaned, holding myself as still as possible to minimise the agony I felt in my skull if I moved. As my eyes adjusted, I gingerly looked around, moving my head as slowly as possible.

Where was I? My heart started racing, and I squeezed my eyes tightly shut, curling into a ball. My breathing grew shallow, and a sob tore from my mouth before I was even aware of it.

I fell apart.

Eventually, my cries turned to whimpers, and I concentrated on breathing slowly and deeply, in through my nose, and out through my mouth. When I finally felt calm enough to take stock of my surroundings without panicking, I raised my head.

It was difficult to make out much. The only light came from a single oval-shaped bulb on the wall to my left, hanging over a wooden door which was slightly ajar. I could feel a very faint breeze blowing in from somewhere, so there must've been a vent or air shaft in this room, although I couldn't see it. Other than that, I was surrounded by solid stone. Floor, walls, and ceiling. No windows. If I had to guess, I'd say I was underground somewhere, possibly in a cellar of some sort. It had that kind of damp, cold feeling. Stone steps in the corner of the room ascended to the ceiling where there was what looked like a hatch opening, and next to the steps was another wooden door with a padlock. I was sitting on a mattress which had a pile of blankets at one end, and there was a small metal table next to the mattress with a bottle of water on it.

I peered at the bottle suspiciously, debating whether it was safe to drink. It didn't *look* like the seal had been tampered with, but I wasn't about to risk it, despite my parched throat. I needed to get out of here.

Flexing my wrists, I climbed to my feet, using the cold stone wall to support me. A wave of dizziness overtook me, and I swayed on my feet, nausea rising up in my throat. *Fuck.* My legs suddenly gave way underneath me, and I crashed back down onto the mattress.

Okay. I wasn't going anywhere. Yet. I pulled my legs up and rested my chin on my knees, closing my eyes until the dizziness passed. How could I stay positive? Was there anything positive? There didn't seem to be any blood coming from my head, at least—I guess I could be grateful for small mercies?

Unfortunately, that thought did nothing to comfort me.

Footsteps sounded overhead, and my heart pounded, drumming loudly in my ears as there was a loud screeching of metal against metal, and the hatch opened, revealing a pair of black shoes.

They stepped onto the first step.

Then the next.

Then the next.

I huddled on the mattress, my back against the wall, biting down on the sleeve of my hoodie to stop myself from doing anything stupid like screaming the fucking place down. I'd never been so terrified in my life, and if I hadn't practically collapsed when I'd tried to stand, I'd have been trying to make a run for it.

A man came into view—short, stocky, pale, dressed in the uniform of a security guard, complete with a black cap. He paused for a moment, closing the hatch behind him, before he descended the rest of the way down the stairs. When he saw I was awake and watching him, his lip curled, and he quickly strode across the floor, grabbing me and pulling to my feet. Another wave of dizziness hit me, and only his arms around me stopped me from falling. He gripped me tightly around the waist, my back to his front.

"What are you doing here, little girl?" He spoke in heavily accented English.

"Little girl? Excuse me!" I spluttered, before clapping my mouth shut. *Don't antagonise the strange man, idiot!*

"One more time." He bent his head close to my ear, his breath smelling faintly of onions, hot on my cheek. *Gross.* "What are you doing here?"

I said the first thing that flew into my mind. "I came to look at the boats."

He chuckled humourlessly. "You are telling me you came to look at the boats, on restricted land, at night?"

"Yep."

"Foolish gi—" His words were cut off by a faint, muffled shout overhead.

"Winter!"

Caiden.

Determination filled me, and I opened my mouth to scream as loudly as I could, but the man slammed his hand across my mouth. In a flash, I felt a cold metal blade at my throat, and I froze in place.

"*Nyet.* Do not move. Do not make a sound. I will take great pleasure in slicing your pretty little throat open."

Who the fuck speaks like this?

He pressed the blade harder against me, and all thoughts flew out of my mind as I felt a sharp sting. Tears rolled silently down my cheeks as I stood, statue still, listening to the faint sounds overhead. Caiden was right there, above me, and I couldn't tell him.

The sounds faded away, and I knew he was gone.

The pressure against my neck disappeared, and the man spun me, throwing me down onto the mattress. My head jerked as I fell, sending a searing pain through me. Black spots danced in front of my eyes, and I struggled to stay conscious.

Dimly, I heard a ringing sound, then the pounding of footsteps as the man ascended the stairs. I heard him bark a string of words into his phone that made no sense to me in my state, followed by the sound of scraping metal assaulting my ears again. I curled up, holding my head, and closed my eyes.

Peeling my eyes open, I became aware of the man from before, sitting on a chair, cigarette in hand, watching me.

When he saw I was awake, he stood, throwing his cigarette to the floor and stubbing it out with his boot.

"Bathroom." He pointed to the door directly under the single light. "Water." He indicated the bottle on the table that I'd noticed before, and then his voice turned threatening and cold. "Do not attempt to leave. You will not like the consequences."

With that threat echoing through the room, he stomped off up the stairs, the hatch slamming down into place behind him.

My throat was so sore that I threw caution to the wind, sitting up slowly and unscrewing the cap of the water bottle. The liquid slid down my parched throat, soothing it, and I drank around a third of the bottle, not knowing when I'd be getting any more.

Once I'd placed the water back on the table, I carefully climbed to my feet, and holding on to the wall for support, made my way to the tiny bathroom, pulling the light cord that dangled from the ceiling. The room contained very little—just an ancient porcelain toilet and a tiny, cracked sink with a tarnished mirror above it.

I examined my throat in the mirror, noticing a thin line of red where the knife had nicked my flesh. Thankfully it only seemed like a minor scratch. Turning on the tap, I put my hands under the brownish-coloured icy water that came spurting out, and when it ran clear, I used my hands to gently clean the cut as much as I could, then dabbed water over my face.

Once that was done and my skin was numb from the cold, I felt my head, where there was a sizeable lump, which sent throbbing pain through me as soon as I touched it. Quickly dropping my hand, I made my way back to the mattress, collapsing down onto it, barely caring about the springs digging into me as another wave of nausea and dizziness overtook me. I pulled one of the blankets from the pile over me, resting my sore head on another, and somehow managed to fall asleep.

I had no idea how much time had passed when I awoke, but my stomach was painfully empty, and I gulped down another third of my water, forcing myself to stop and save some for later. I wasn't sure if the tap water was safe to drink, and the last thing I needed was to get ill on top of everything else.

What to do? I was in no state to try to escape, with my head all fucked up, but I had to try something. A slow circuit of the room proved fruitless—the other door next to the stairs had a heavy-duty padlock that I had no way of opening. I stood next to the stairs, leaning against the wall, trying to get my brain in gear so I could think. My only chance was to make a run for it when the man returned next. Could I even run in this state? I had to try.

Mind made up, I decided to try the classic trick of arranging my blankets in a lump in the hope it would look like there was a body under there. Obviously there was no way it would actually fool him up close, but it might buy me enough time to get up the stairs and out...where? My guess was that I was still at the docks. I had to take it one step at a time. First, get out and find a hiding place, then take it from there.

I arranged my blankets and turned on the bathroom light, leaving the door ajar, so that if the blanket trick failed straight away, he might think I was in the bathroom. Yeah, it was a pretty horrendous, flimsy plan, but it was the only one I had.

Hiding in the shadows by the stairs, I waited.

The scraping of metal echoed through the room, and the throbbing in my head increased at the sound. I battled another wave of dizziness—there was no way I was going to let anything stop my escape attempt.

Footsteps descended the stairs, and once they hit the floor, I counted to five under my breath, then made a run for it. Scrambling up the stairs as fast as I could go, my ears ringing and my heart pounding, I reached out with my hands to touch the pitted metal surface of the hatch opening.

My fingers made contact, and at the same time I was grabbed around the legs and yanked downwards, my cheek smacking into cold stone as my face connected with one of the steps. Arms caught me, and I felt a sharp jab in my neck.

I knew nothing else.

4

caiden

Two and a half days.

Sixty hours, give or take.

No Winter.

The four of us were going insane. Kinslee was blowing up our phones, wanting to know where she was. We'd told her Winter was ill and would be in contact when she was better—anything to delay her while we searched.

"Anything?" I asked Weston for the tenth time, and he shook his head, frustration clear in his eyes.

"Nothing."

None of our contacts had been able to find any trace of Winter. Best-case scenario, she was still at the docks, and we'd somehow missed something important. Worst case—she'd ended up on the *Argo Navis*, which we still knew fuck all about. Or...no. I wouldn't let my mind consider anything else.

Down in the basement gym, West and I spotted each other on the weights, both of us trying to focus on anything but the problem of Winter going missing. I'd never felt so fucking helpless in my life. Every minute we went without answers was another minute where she could be in danger, or worse.

"Car. Now." Zayde burst into the gym, where I'd just started pummelling the punchbag, needing to take out my frustrations on something. Weston sat up from the weights bench, grabbing a towel, his eyes widening as he took in Zayde's expression.

"What is it?"

"Docks," he threw over his shoulder, already heading back up the stairs, and my stomach lurched.

Cassius pulled up in the same place we'd stopped last time, behind a black-and-chrome motorbike with a guy standing next to it. Lloyd "Mack" Mackenzie. An intimidating-looking fucker—shaved head, tatted up, dressed in bike leathers, a black bandana covering the lower part of his face. His dark eyes swung to us before his attention zeroed in on Zayde.

Zayde climbed out and went to speak to him, talking in low tones, then beckoned us over.

Mack met my eyes as I came to a stop in front of him. "Rich boy." I nodded at him, clenching and unclenching my fists, on edge. He must've read the impatience in my eyes because he got to the point straight away. "The security guard was overheard arguing with someone on the phone earlier—another one of Creed's boys was keeping an eye out. He didn't catch the conversation, but he heard the guard say something about 'holding the girl captive.' Someone turned up at the gate, waiting to be let out, and he had to get out of there."

He grabbed his helmet from the bike seat and straddled the bike. "I came by to check it out after hours, and the security guard is nowhere to be seen. Been watching the place for the last hour, and there's no sign of him. If you want another look round, now's your chance."

I didn't wait to hear any more. I ran towards the docks, Z, Cass and West right alongside me, as the bike roared off behind us.

We reached the empty guard hut, and Weston went straight to the camera feeds. "Gate camera's still on the blink." He shrugged. "Makes life easier. Just avoid these areas." He cycled through the feeds, indicating the spaces the working cameras were pointing at, mostly facing the water.

"Let's start at the building where we found Winter's phone," Cass suggested.

"Yeah. That's what I think, too." Fuck, my voice was coming out all hoarse. I gritted my teeth. We'd find her. There was no other option.

Stalking down the same corridor as before, I came to an abrupt halt, Cassius running into my back.

"Cade!" Weston's harsh whisper-shout sounded close to my ear.

"I see it," I muttered.

We stood over the body lying on the floor in front of us. I nudged it with my foot, carefully flipping it over.

I took in the details—a short, stocky guy, shaved head, a crooked nose, dressed in a black shirt and trousers, with a radio clipped to his belt. As I moved him, my eyes were drawn to the area just above his ear. The whole side of his head was caved in, a pool of blood spreading underneath. An iron bar lay discarded a few feet away, stained red.

The smell of blood filled the air, a coppery, metallic tang, catching in my throat.

I hoped like fuck that this blood only belonged to the

dead guy. Winter…no. She was going to be okay. There was no other option.

Weston made a gagging sound, turning away. Zayde stared impassively at the body, then pulled out his phone.

"I need another favour… Yeah. Clean-up crew… Same place."

He ended the call. "I'm going to meet the others. Check the rest of the building."

"I'm going with him. I need some fresh air." Weston scrubbed a hand across his face, blowing out a breath, then disappeared back down the corridor. I stood, still staring down at the body, trying to process everything. What the fuck had happened here?

Cassius came to stand beside me. "He'll never get a chance to get ahead in life, now," he commented, using the toe of his shoe to point to the dead guy's skull.

Twisting around, I stared at him.

"Get it? Ahead? His head?"

I raised a brow. "Really. You got jokes, now?"

"I've always got jokes." He shrugged.

"Right…" I cleared my throat. "Get *your* head in the game. Come on."

We started walking down the corridor, avoiding the pool of blood that had spread around the body.

"Cade!"

My brother's urgent shout from the doorway sent me spinning around, and I was standing in front of him before I was even aware I'd moved. "What? Is it Winter?"

He handed me his phone. "It's Kinslee."

Kinslee? I held the phone to my ear. "What?"

"Caiden. Fuck. I'm so glad I got hold of you guys." Her voice was shaky. "I'm…I'm at the hospital. With Winter. Not the local hospital; I'm at Lansdown General. Can you come?"

Winter. "On my way," I said brusquely, then ended the call, handing the phone to Weston. "Let's go. Winter's at Lansdown General Hospital."

She was in hospital.

With Kinslee.

Safe.

I fucking hoped.

"Why not the local hospital? What the fuck is going on?"

I had no answer for Cassius. And at the moment, I didn't care. I needed Winter to be okay. That was the only thing on my mind.

We pulled into the hospital car park forty minutes later, and West called Kinslee to find out where to go. After getting lost following her instructions, we eventually ended up in the waiting room of a large ward, all white, sterile walls, and blue padded chairs with metal frames.

Kinslee appeared in the corridor, her hair pulled back, dressed in yoga pants and a thick jumper. She crooked a finger at us, exhaustion clear in her face.

I raced over to her. "Where is she?" I didn't bother with pleasantries—I needed to see Winter. Now.

"Come on." I followed her down the corridor to a small, private room. She opened the door.

Snowflake.

Whoever did this to her was going to fucking pay.

5

winter

I blinked my eyes open, wincing at the bright light.

Everything hurt.

I slipped back into the darkness.

"Water." I croaked the word, my voice hoarse and cracked from disuse. I squinted, the room slowly coming into focus.

"Winter." Kinslee leaned into me, her amber eyes full of concern.

"Hi," I whispered.

She stared at me, relief clear in her gaze. "How are you feeling?" She handed me a paper cup brimming with cool liquid, and I eagerly gulped it down, letting it soothe my parched throat.

"Okay. I think." I continued to whisper, still weak and in pain. Fuck, my head hurt, so much.

My eyes were drawn to a chair in the corner of the room, a familiar presence dominating the space, despite him being asleep.

"He's been here almost the whole time. Ever since I called him. The others brought him a change of clothes and whatever, but he's barely left your side, except when he's been forced to."

My stomach flipped. He'd stayed with me?

"All of the Four have been here, on and off." Kinslee's eyes sparkled. "Your room is incredibly popular with the nurses."

"I can't imagine why," I managed to husk out.

I groaned, the pain overtaking me again, spots dancing in front of my eyes. The blackness pulled me under.

The next time I woke up, I felt almost normal, other than the pounding pain in my skull and a throbbing in my cheek. The first thing I saw was Caiden. His head rested on my bed, his thick, raven hair close to my fingertips. I stretched out my hand, running it through the soft strands. Was I dreaming?

His head shot up from the bed.

"Snowflake?"

"Yes." I breathed out the word, attempting to pull him closer to me, with whatever amount of strength I had left.

"Fuck." His voice cracked, and he gathered me in his arms, so carefully it made me catch my breath. What was going on?

I was surrounded by him. All powerful male, his presence strong and reassuring. He kissed my head softly, his arms tightening around me.

What?

This wasn't Caiden. He didn't act like this.

I must be dreaming.

I let oblivion overtake me.

"So, how long have you worked here?"

I awoke, completely conscious, my mind more or less clear. Kinslee was seated on a plastic chair next to me, her eyes on a good-looking male nurse who was checking the clear bag that was connected to my arm by a long tube.

"Morning," I croaked, and both their heads snapped round to me. I smirked at the identical expressions of shock on their faces.

"You're awake. I'll get the doctor," the nurse mumbled, rushing out of the room.

"Kins? What's going on?"

"You had an...accident. Don't tell the doctors anything," she hissed urgently. "We'll get to the bottom of this afterwards, okay?"

"Yep." I agreed, my senses on high alert. As high as they could be, anyway, after dragging myself out of unconsciousness. "Is there any water? My throat hurts."

Kinslee stood. "Yeah, there's a dispenser just outside. I'll get you some." As she disappeared out of the room, I noticed Weston huddled in a chair in the corner, asleep. A memory flashed through my mind—Caiden asleep in that same chair. Then...Caiden next to my bed, pulling me into his arms. Did I dream that, or did it really happen?

As if that thought had unlocked something in my mind, memory after memory came flooding back to me. Being knocked out. The cold, dark basement. My captor.

My breath caught in my throat.

I gasped. My heart rate kicked up, sending the monitor I was attached to crazy, and a nurse came rushing in. I made an effort to slow my heart rate, breathing deeply in and out, silently counting from one to ten and blocking everything else from my mind. The nurse checked my blood pressure and monitored my heart rate on the machine for a few minutes before leaving, satisfied that I was okay. Kinslee, who had appeared back in the room during my panic episode, handed me a plastic cup of water, and I drank it gratefully.

I stayed mostly silent as various doctors and nurses came in and out of the room throughout the day, running checks, asking me questions I had no answer for. Throughout it all, one of the Four was always with me, a constant, silent presence that the medical staff were unable to persuade to leave.

Eventually they agreed to let me go after a night of observation—I was okay, medically, and as a legal adult, they couldn't keep me there any longer. Since I'd had a mild concussion, apparently, I was lectured on self-care and given a list of all the fun things I shouldn't do in the near future—including skiing, skydiving and riding a motorbike (sorry, Zayde). Not that any of the things they mentioned to me were likely to happen, especially not now, when I had way more important priorities to worry about.

The next day, as Kinslee led me to the car where Cassius was waiting, she told me I'd been out of it for five days.

Five days.

My mind whirling, I walked next to Kinslee, almost on autopilot, her hand a gentle but firm grip on my arm. The crisp, fresh air on my face was welcome after all the time I'd spent cooped up inside.

We reached the car park, and my eyes were drawn straight to the hulking, matte-black SUV where a tall, gorgeous man with dirty-blond hair waited, casually leaning against the car door, twirling his keys around on his finger. As we approached him, a smile appeared on his face, but worry was clear in his gaze as he watched me.

Cassius.

As happy as I was to see him, and I was happy, I wished more than anything that waiting alongside him had been a certain raven-haired, brooding man with stormy eyes.

We reached the car, and Cassius moved from where he leaned against the door to draw me into a hug. "How you doing?" he murmured into my ear.

"I'm alright. Thanks, Cass."

His voice dropped even further. "You gave us all a scare. Cade, more than anyone."

"Sorry," I whispered, twisting my head to look at him and giving him a wry smile. "I couldn't really help it."

"Don't be sorry. Just...don't do anything that reckless again, okay?"

"I'll try not to."

He tutted, shaking his head at me, and opened the passenger door. "Let's get you home."

I felt like an invalid as Cassius and Kinslee fussed around me, settling me into the passenger seat. Kinslee reached across me and snapped my seat belt into place, before hopping into the back of the car.

As Cassius started the engine, I pulled down the sun visor to see just how bad I looked.

Yeah. I shouldn't have bothered looking. I groaned as I took in the greenish-yellow bruising mottling my cheek, dark against my pale skin. Stretching my neck gingerly, I examined my throat, noting that the cut was almost completely healed, just the faintest line remaining.

I twisted in my seat, meeting Kinslee's eyes. "What happened to me?"

Silence reigned.

"Kinslee Stewart, you'd better start talking, right now."

I wasn't expecting her laugh, low and bitter.

"Oh, like you told me what was going on with you? Like you just decided to keep your bestie in the dark? You couldn't fucking trust me, huh?"

Shit.

"Kins," Cass warned in a low tone, meeting her eyes in the rear-view mirror and giving a small shake of his head.

I stared at her, trying to gauge her mood. Pissed off, and hurt, if I had to guess. Did I take a risk and trust her?

I took a leap of faith.

"When we get back to the house, I'll tell you everything."

We pulled up to the Four's house, and I gingerly stepped from the car, rubbing at my head as the ache intensified.

Silently, I followed Cassius up to the front door, Kinslee gripping my arm once again. As we entered the wide hallway, a blast of heat hit me, welcome after the chill outside. Kinslee placed my bag just inside the door, and I stood with her for a moment, tension I hadn't realised I was holding seeping out of me. I felt safe here. I *was* safe.

"We'll be in the kitchen," Kinslee muttered, her eyes flicking to the stairs. Then she tugged on Cassius' arm, giving him a pointed look, and they disappeared off down the hallway.

I turned to look, the pounding in my head forgotten as I saw him.

Standing partway up the staircase, a black T-shirt stretched across his torso, faded, ripped jeans low on his hips, he stared at me silently, his gaze impenetrable. I tracked his movements as he descended the stairs, coming closer and closer until he was standing right in front of me.

I stared into his stormy eyes, noticing the dark circles, the way his hair was all tousled like he'd been pulling at it, the stubble darkening his jaw.

"Cade," I whispered hoarsely, and my whole body started trembling, tears filling my eyes and spilling down my cheeks as I broke apart in front of him.

He closed his eyes briefly, scrubbing a hand across his face, before his gaze met mine again. "Snowflake." His voice was just as hoarse as mine as he reached down and took my hand, gently tugging me towards the stairs.

I just wanted him to hold me. To tell me everything would be okay. I could barely see through the haze of tears as I stumbled up the stairs, one hand encased by his, and the other gripping the banister, letting it take my weight.

We ended up in his room, and he sat on the bed. "Come here," he commanded, and I was finally, *finally* in his arms. He cradled my body, breathing into my hair, as I hugged him tightly and let his solid presence soothe me until I was finally calm.

Drawing back, I looked at him, and he finally let his mask drop. His eyes swirled with a mix of worry, hurt, and relief, but I could see the anger simmering just under the surface. With a rush, the whole situation with James came back to me, and I gasped, needing to explain, needing to know if we were okay.

"Caiden—"

He cut me off with a forceful kiss.

I opened my mouth for him, kissing him back just as aggressively, manoeuvring myself without breaking the kiss so I was straddling him, running my hands over the hard planes of his muscles and up to the back of his neck. He groaned into my mouth, his hands sliding up to tangle in my hair as he took my breath away.

I winced, and he immediately pulled back, both of us breathing heavily, our eyes locked.

"What's wrong?"

"My head. It started hurting again."

"Shit. I'm sorry, I didn't think." He brushed my hair back from my face, his gaze full of concern.

"It's not your fault. I wanted to kiss you."

Lifting his hand, he traced the pad of his fingers carefully across the bruise on my cheek, his eyes darkening. "I want to kill whoever did this to you."

My stomach flipped. "I'm okay. It's okay. Everything's going to be okay."

I didn't know who I was trying to reassure more—him, or myself.

He lowered his hand and carefully moved me so I was sitting sideways on top of him. "What do you want to do? Do you want to rest? To talk to the others?"

The pain in my head intensified. "Rest, please." I clambered off him, crawling up the bed until I collapsed with my head on his pillow. "Will you stay with me?" My eyes were already closed.

I felt him move, and then his body was next to mine, his arm draped across me.

"I'm not going anywhere." He kissed my forehead, pulling me closer. "We need to talk when you're up to it." His voice was soft, but I could hear the intent and meaning in his tone.

I sighed. "I know."

Sleep pulled me under.

6

winter

When I woke, the sun was high in the sky, streaming through the window. I turned my head to see Caiden sitting up against the headboard, engrossed in whatever he was doing on his phone.

"Hi."

His head shot up and he met my gaze, his lips tipping up into a small smile. "Feeling better?"

"I think so." The pain had dulled to a low ache, nothing that couldn't be fixed by the painkillers the hospital pharmacy had provided me with when I'd been discharged.

Pulling myself into a seated position, I turned to face him. "Look, I know we have things to discuss. I also need someone to fill in the blanks for me—how I ended up in hospital, and..." My voice trailed off at the sound of pounding footsteps, and suddenly the door was thrown open and Weston was barrelling towards me, pulling me up and off the bed and into his arms.

"Winter," he ground out thickly, holding me so tightly I was in danger of asphyxiation. He rained kisses down on my head, and I smiled against his chest even as I struggled to get air into my lungs.

"West," I mumbled, tapping on his back, and he drew back from me, his teal-blue eyes full of emotion, meeting mine. "Thanks. I couldn't breathe." I smiled to let him know I was joking, and he returned my smile.

"Are you okay? How's your head? Your bruise looks loads better today."

Better? How bad did it look before? "I'm fine," I reassured him. "Nothing that a couple of painkillers won't sort out."

"Good." Giving me a final squeeze, he released me, and Caiden stood, sliding his arm around my waist.

"You wanna talk to everyone at the same time so we only have to go through this once?"

I nodded. "Sounds good to me. I'm dying for a shower first, though. My hair is gross."

"We'll wait here, in case you need anything. Keep the door unlocked," Caiden told me, walking me over to the bathroom door as if I couldn't walk there myself. "Or I can come in and help?"

I laughed. "I'm fine. I'll be quick."

Feeling much fresher after my shower, my hair finally clean again, I rejoined Caiden and Weston in the bedroom, and together, the three of us made our way downstairs into the kitchen, where Kinslee, Zayde, and Cassius waited.

Weston crossed to the table, and Caiden sauntered over to the fridge, pulling out a can of Coke. He turned to me, raising a questioning brow, and I nodded, and he reached in to grab another can for me.

Kinslee flashed me a quick smile from her seat at the table, and Cassius moved from where he leaned against the large black marble island, to draw me into a hug. "Good to see you up and about."

"Thanks. For the lift from the hospital, too."

"That's what friends are for, babe." He kissed the top of my head, then let me go, crossing over to the kitchen table, where he sank into a chair next to Weston.

Zayde remained where he was, next to the island, his sharp gaze assessing me. I bit my lip, uncomfortable with his stare, but forced myself to hold his gaze. After the longest thirty seconds of my life, our silent stare-off ended as I blinked, and a smirk played across his full lips. "Good to see you in one piece." He stepped towards me and leaned down to kiss my non-bruised cheek, his stubble grazing my skin.

I gaped at him, and then my attention was diverted by a glint of silver. "You got another piercing?" I was positive I hadn't seen the small stud in the... "What's that bit of your ear called?"

"Helix." He stared at me for a moment, then leaned closer, his voice low, the words sounding like they'd been dragged out of him. "I had to do *something*."

"What do you mean?" I asked, mystified, but he'd already drawn away, striding quickly around the table as if he had to put as much distance between us as possible. Shaking my head, I chalked it up to another one of the many things I didn't understand about him and made my way to join the others. I sank down into a chair next to Caiden, and he handed me my can of Coke. Opening it, I took a large swig, savouring the cool, sweet fizz as it slid down my throat, then placing the can back on the table, I looked around at the Four and Kinslee.

I needed to know what had happened to me. The last thing I remembered before waking up in hospital was being pulled back as I tried to escape. I chewed my lip, my heart racing as everything came flooding back to me once more—

the darkness, the fear, and the sudden rush of pain before I became completely numb.

Gripping the sides of my chair, the smooth, solid wood under my fingers bringing me back to the present, I slowed my breathing, doing my trick of counting to ten silently. Once I'd gathered myself and was sure my voice would remain steady, I spoke. "Who wants to be the first to fill me in?"

Kinslee took a deep breath. "I guess I'll start, since I got to you first. Not that I know much"—she glared at Caiden before returning her gaze to mine—"since no one would tell me anything. I had a phone call telling me that you'd had an accident, and to come straight to the hospital. I panicked—you'd told me you were going to see the Four, and I thought..." Her voice trailed off as she swallowed hard, visibly trying to compose herself.

"Hey, it's okay." I reached out and grabbed her hand. "Who called you?"

"The hospital."

"So, how did I get there?"

She shrugged. "I don't know. All the hospital would tell me was that you'd been 'dropped off'—they didn't know who had brought you there."

I stared at her, my brow furrowed. "How come they called you, anyway?"

"Your student ID card. I guess they got hold of the university, and I'm listed as your emergency contact." Leaning closer to me, she lowered her voice a little. "You scared me, with the way you looked. I didn't know what to do, so I phoned Weston. Then the next thing I know, three of them are at the hospital with me, taking over. They wouldn't leave you, especially with no one knowing what had happened, if there was still a threat. We couldn't risk your safety. I stayed with you, too, as much as I could."

"Thank you," I whispered, squeezing her hand. Why hadn't I confided in her sooner? "I owe you an explanation, and maybe I'd better do it before the boys give me their part of the story." I glanced over at Caiden, and he nodded, once.

"Okay. Well, it all started with my dad..."

I told her the entire story, holding nothing back—why I'd come to Alstone, the reason the Four had been so hostile to me to begin with, and our suspicions about my mother. Throughout it all, Kinslee sat, a stunned expression on her face, her eyes filling with tears as I spoke about my dad, widening as I recounted meeting Petr, and then narrowing in anger as I got to the final part, where I'd stupidly decided to go to the docks alone.

"If you weren't so bruised still, I'd throttle you for being so careless with your own safety. Seriously, Winter. You're lucky that nothing worse happened to you."

"Kins. Not now." Cass frowned at her, and she sat back in her seat with a huff.

The Four took it in turns to recount their side of the events, glossing over the details of their evening at Alstone Members Club, and concentrating on how they'd received my message when they'd left, and come to find me straight away. I added how I'd driven to the docks and seen the boat and the three figures, and someone had hit me over the head.

When I recounted my time in the basement room, and my experience with my captor, the atmosphere in the room grew strained, to put it mildly. Caiden pulled me onto him and banded his arms around my waist, tension rolling off him in waves. Zayde flicked his knife open and closed, over and over, his jaw clenched, and Weston stood, pacing up and down, his eyes darkening. His expressive face showed everything he was feeling—fury, worry, helplessness—they were all there.

"What we need to know now is, what the fuck is going on at the docks." Cassius slammed his hand down on the table, making me jump, and my head started pounding again.

"And more importantly, who hurt Winter," Caiden said in a low voice, close to my ear, speaking through gritted teeth. "Make them fucking pay."

"I don't know how we're going to get those answers. Just add it to the ever-growing pile of questions." I sighed, rubbing my temples.

"You've got me to help, now. If you'll have me." Kinslee spoke up. "I don't know how much I can do, but from everything you've told me, I can't sit back. I need to help. I could always speak to my brother, since he worked at the docks last summer?"

"That's not a bad idea, y'know." West flashed her a grin, and she smiled back, pleased.

"How do you feel about looking at gory pictures?" Z suddenly asked me out of nowhere.

"Huh? What do you mean?" I frowned, turning to face him.

"My contact forwarded me a photo of the dead guy we found at the docks. His face is...damaged..." he said, carefully. "But if you can cope with the blood and gore, you might be able to work out if it's the same guy that held you captive."

"If it helps us, I'll look."

He nodded, sliding his phone across the table to me.

Fuuuuck.

Damaged was *so* not the word I'd use.

My stomach rolled as I studied the image of the body, his head completely smashed in, his face almost unrecognisable. Steeling myself, I zoomed in on the photo, trying to avoid looking at the worst bits, concentrating on the intact parts.

"I can't be a hundred percent sure, but I think that's him. The hair is the same. And what I can see of the clothes."

"So if that's him, who rescued you?" Kinslee spoke the question I was sure we were all wondering.

"Another one to add to the list." I shrugged, sliding the phone back to Zayde.

As if the nausea from looking at that image wasn't enough, a sudden zing of pain shot through my head, and I bit my lip to stifle a groan. Caiden didn't miss it, though. "You need your painkillers," he stated. Moving me back to my own seat, he pushed back his chair, the legs scraping against the floor, and headed out of the kitchen. He reappeared a couple of minutes later with two tablets, which I swallowed with my Coke.

"I need to rest. Sorry, I feel really wiped out." I rubbed my head again. "I thought I was okay, but I guess not."

"You can't expect to recover that quickly. You had a traumatic head injury, not to mention all that bruising on your face. You were out of it for almost five days straight." Cass gave me a severe look. "We're not gonna let you do anything except rest and recover, until you're back to normal."

"But—"

He held up a hand. "Sorry, we already agreed. Kinslee, too."

I swallowed hard around the lump in my throat. They really did care about me. In such a short space of time, the people in this room had become the most important people in my life. “Thanks,” I managed to say.

“C’mon.” Caiden pulled me to my feet, and we headed into the lounge, where he set me up on the sofa under a blanket. He then crossed to the door and spoke to someone on the other side, then closed it firmly behind us.

Time to have the conversation I’d been dreading. I could only hope that Caiden believed me.

7

winter

Returning to me, Caiden sank down next to me on the sofa and turned to meet my eyes, his stormy gaze troubled, torn between concern and the clear need to know what had gone down with me and James. "You up to talking? I asked the others to leave us alone for a while."

"Yeah. Listen, I was in the library, and James tried to kiss me. I pushed him away as soon as I recovered from the shock. I don't know what's going on, but..." My voice trailed off as I stared at him. "Cade? You do believe me, don't you?"

He scrubbed a hand across his face, and the hesitation before he answered told me everything. Everything I didn't want to hear.

He exhaled heavily, staring straight ahead. "I want to. I mean, I do. Look, you have to understand how fucking bad that video looked. I see my girl all over Granville, hugging him and touching his face, then the next minute, you're kissing him."

"Are you serious right now? Don't you trust me?" I

couldn't help the frustration, and yeah, anger, that bled through my tone.

He was silent for a long moment, his eyes meeting mine again, just looking at me, letting his walls down so I could see the torment in his eyes. A pain started in my chest, spreading the longer he remained silent, and I dug my nails into my palms to give myself something to concentrate on to stop myself from crying.

"Fuck...Winter. It's not— I find it hard to trust," he finally admitted in a low, defeated voice, and my eyes filled with tears.

"Caiden. Do you want to be with me? Like in a real relationship?" I leaned closer to him, watching him intently as all his emotions played out on his face.

"Yeah."

A tear rolled down my cheek. "If we don't have trust, what do we have? How can we have a relationship if you won't let yourself trust me?"

He closed his eyes, his jaw tightening. "I don't know. Fuck."

I steeled myself. It was clear he needed to get things straight in his own head. "I-I think we should take a step back and re-evaluate things. Just be friends for now. Maybe it's better if we just concentrate on getting to the bottom of whatever's going on with my mother."

His eyes flew open, and he looked at me, his expression shuttered. "If that's what you want."

"It's not what I want, but if you can't trust me, we can't have anything real, or solid." Somehow I managed to get the words out without my voice cracking, even though they broke me to say them. I'd thought he trusted me, especially since he'd told me about his mum, something that was personal and clearly still haunted him. Maybe he'd even thought he trusted me. I could deal with his possessiveness, and his jealousy, but now the incident with James had happened, and if he was doubting what I was telling him, then it proved just how fragile that trust was.

If he couldn't trust me, then we couldn't be together.

"*Fuck*." He took a deep breath, bringing his hands up to cup my face. "Listen. I want you, but I can't help the way I feel." Clenching his jaw, he bit out, "I still feel fucking rage every time I think of his hands on you. You've got history together. Rationally, I know you're not lying to me, but…" He trailed off and shrugged helplessly.

"Okay. I can't do anything more to change your mind, you know that, right? *You* need to decide you can trust me." I leaned forward, kissing him softly on the lips, trying so hard not to lose it, my vision clouding as my eyes filled with tears. "Friends, then? For now?"

"I…" He sighed, defeated. "I guess so, yeah." His voice was low and unhappy. "Friends it is." He ran his thumb lightly across my cheek, placed a kiss to the bruise that was still prominent on my cheekbone, then he got to his feet. "I'm sorry, Snowflake," he gritted out, and then he was gone.

As soon as the door closed behind him, I breathed in and out deeply, counting under my breath, suppressing the misery that was trying to rise to the surface. I didn't want to give anyone yet another reason to worry about my well-being.

And I still held out hope.

Hope that Caiden would realise that he could trust me. Maybe this would be the push he needed. Somehow, that broody man had worked his way under my skin, and I couldn't give up on him. On us.

Weston sauntered into the room, took one look at my

face, and his own face fell. “Do you need me to kick the shit out of my brother?”

I snorted, despite myself. “You think you could take him?”

“Easy.” He winked at me, then flopped down on the sofa and lifted his arm. “C’mere.” I curled into his side and relaxed against him, listening to his steady heartbeat, letting him soothe me. Kinslee joined us, sitting on my other side. She was quickly followed by Cassius, who grabbed the remote, and soon we were all engrossed in a movie. I felt safe here, in this secure house, with the Four and Kinslee. Right here, right now, I could pretend that everything was normal, that we were just friends spending time together, without any threats or danger hanging over us.

Tomorrow would come soon enough, but we’d face it. Together.

8

winter

Not even three days later, and I'd temporarily moved into the Four's house—into the guest room, to be exact. Not out of choice. If I'd thought it was bad when they were shadowing me everywhere before I really knew them, it was nothing compared to now. One of them accompanied me everywhere anytime I left the house.

They'd offered Kinslee a place to stay, too, but she was adamant that she'd be fine. I felt guilty, leaving her alone, but she'd brushed my concerns aside.

Still, I made sure that the hacked feed from the cameras facing her apartment building was monitored regularly, and Weston had installed his security app on her phone.

I was sitting with Weston in what I still called the "spy room," playing with my shiny new phone. It had turned up in a box on my bed when I'd moved in. No note, but I had a feeling that Caiden may have been responsible. He hadn't said anything, but I'd caught his pleased grin when he'd seen the phone in my hand, when we were all hanging out on the first night I'd stayed with the Four.

Dragging my attention from my phone screen, I focused on Weston as he showed me how to select and enlarge the various camera feeds, when his phone buzzed with a message. Glancing at it, his whole body tensed, and he leaned forwards, typing furiously on the keyboard until the image in front of him was replaced with a blank screen with a blinking cursor in the top right corner.

"What are you doing?"

He typed in a string of letters and symbols that made no sense to me, and a login screen appeared. "Dark web. Mercury wants to speak to me."

Mercury. My heart skipped a beat, and I hoped with everything in me that this meant he had information for us.

"I might be a while. You wanna get a drink, or something?" He flashed me a quick smile, before returning his focus to the screen.

"Good idea." I left him to it, knowing how engrossed he'd be and trusting him to update me with everything afterwards. Heading into the lounge, I picked up my own laptop and started working on an assignment I was partway through. I couldn't concentrate, though. I'd been cooped up in this house for the past two days, and after I'd managed to write a grand total of five words after staring blankly at the screen for fifteen minutes, I closed the laptop lid with a bang.

I had to get out of here. Get some fresh air. Go somewhere.

"Winter." Zayde appeared in the doorway, leaning on the wooden frame, the shiny red helmet I'd worn on his bike before dangling from his fingers. His voice was slightly muffled by the skull bandana covering his mouth, and I raised a brow. "Coming?" He threw the helmet to me, then strolled away without a backwards glance.

"Where are we going?" I jumped to my feet, hurrying after him, no idea where we were going, but the need to get out of the house overrode everything else. He didn't answer me, of course, just stopped to grab his own helmet and leather jacket from next to the front door.

I picked up my jacket, zipping it up tightly and lifted the helmet to place it over my head. Then I remembered.

"Z?" He turned his head to face me, his gaze blank, as usual. "I don't think it's a good idea for me to go on your bike. Um...the doctor said I shouldn't do stuff like that until I was recovered." He didn't respond, and I hurried to continue. "I mean, I think I'm fine, now. I just... I probably shouldn't risk it."

His expression didn't change, but he dropped the helmet he was holding onto the console table by the door, and swiped Caiden's car keys from the hook on the wall. I followed his lead, placing my own helmet down, and heading out of the front door behind him.

Flying along the coast road in Caiden's Audi R8, I felt the tension drain from me as I revelled in the feeling of freedom. Yeah, it was an illusion at best, but at this moment in time, I was making the most of it.

The car slowed as we neared a turning onto a small road that sloped down to a car park, next to a small sandy beach littered with pebbles. We came to a stop at the bottom, facing the road, and Zayde unclipped his seatbelt, turning to look out of the window. I followed suit, pushing my dark sunglasses up on top of my head.

"Now what?"

He remained facing the road. "We wait."

Exiting the R8, I took a seat on the low stone wall that edged the car park, dangling my feet over the edge, watching the sea lapping against the rocks. I'd only ever seen it angrily clashing against the cliff face—here, though, it felt calmer, less deadly. I turned to watch Zayde as he climbed out of the car, then prowled around aimlessly, kicking up dust and small stones with his boots, his bandana pulled down and a joint dangling from his lips.

His head shot up as the low purr of an engine sounded, and I followed his line of sight, spinning to face the road as a large black SUV rumbled down the slope and came to a stop in front of him.

The passenger window rolled down, and Zayde flicked away the stub of his joint, grinding the remains under his boot, and leaned into the car, effectively blocking my view before I could catch a glimpse of the occupants. He spoke in a low voice for a few minutes, then stepped back as the driver's-side door opened.

A hooded figure climbed out, tall and intimidating. I could barely make out his face under the hood, the dusky sky making it even harder, but then he started heading towards me, and I launched to my feet, brushing the grit from my palms.

"This is new." The stranger pushed back his hood enough to expose his features. My eyes flew to his—glittering, almost golden in colour and framed with thick lashes, popping against his rich bronze skin. A small scar ran across his left cheekbone, although I barely noticed it, his bright gaze holding me captive.

As I studied him, his lips curved into a grin, softening his harsh features. "Z never brought a girl before. You must be the one causing all the trouble, I take it?"

I returned his grin with a wry smile. "Yeah, you could say that. I'm Winter, Winter Huntington."

"Creed." He clasped my hand briefly, then stepped away. "I've got news for you."

Who was he? My gaze darted between him and Zayde, but I kept my mouth shut as he continued.

"We couldn't ID the body, but we have this." He handed Zayde a clear Ziploc bag, which he quickly pocketed, but not before I saw a flash of red and the gleam of something metallic inside. "My boys have been keeping eyes on the docks, but security's been stepped up since the guard went missing. As far as we know, no one knows you were there, and I suggest you keep it that way. Lay low for a while, yeah?"

Zayde nodded once. "Cheers. Appreciate it."

Creed inclined his head, then started backing towards his car. "We'll be in touch if we find anything else." He called to me as he reached his door. "Winter. Pleasure to meet you."

I gave him an awkward wave/salute thing, mentally rolling my eyes at myself, then turned back to Caiden's R8. Once we were both settled in our seats, Zayde powered up the engine, and we left the car park behind, speeding along the darkening roads, back towards Alstone.

"House meeting in five." Cassius poked his head around the door frame of the kitchen, where I was finishing up my assignment, perched on a stool at the island, Spotify playing softly in the background.

"House meeting?"

Cassius nodded. "Yeah, Got to divide up the chores."

"What?" I stared at him, confused.

"Not really. We pay people to do the chores. All the cleaning shit, anyway." He gave me a cheeky grin, and I was reminded of how different our lives were. Or not, I guess, since I now lived here for the foreseeable future.

“I’m always happy to do my share of everything. You know that.” Swinging myself off the stool, I picked up my glass of water, ready to head into the lounge.

“Yeah, I know. I’m only fucking with you.” Cassius watched as I came to a halt in front of him, then pulled me into a hug, sending my water sloshing out of the side of my glass and onto his bare chest. “Fuck, that’s cold.” He shivered, laughing and pulling me closer, rubbing his torso into me so my top soaked up the droplets.

“Thanks for that.” I rolled my eyes. “You know, you could consider wearing a T-shirt or something.”

“Nah, I wouldn’t want to deprive anyone the pleasure of seeing this body.” He flexed his pecs, making me laugh, then tugged me towards the lounge, keeping me tucked under his arm. We entered the room, still laughing, and I came to a sudden stop when I saw Caiden sitting on the sofa, staring at us. His face was impassive, but I could see the tight set of his jaw and his stiff posture. Swallowing hard, I ducked under Cassius’ arm and crossed over to Caiden, throwing myself down next to him.

Things between us since the whole conversation where we decided to take a step back and just be friends had been…not awkward, exactly, but we were pretty much tiptoeing around each other, on our best behaviour. Okay, yeah, it was totally awkward. And so difficult. I couldn’t magically turn off my feelings, and all I wanted was to be with him. The rest of the Four, and Kinslee, had been given a heads-up, but it was obvious to me that they didn’t take it seriously. They were still pretty much acting like we were together—well, acting like they were waiting for us to get back together, at least. Okay, *I* was waiting and hoping for the same thing to happen.

Sitting next to him now, his thigh pressed against mine, sent shivers up and down my body, my breath growing shallow as he leaned in to whisper in my ear.

"I fucking hate this," he rasped.

"Me too." My voice was the barest whisper as I turned to look at him. "I just—I need to know you trust me."

He bent his head closer to mine, his breath skating across my lips. "I know." It would have been so easy to lean forwards and kiss him. Was I making a mistake in saying we should just be friends? Should I try to provoke him into action?

Before I could lose myself in my own head, Caiden was moving away from me, leaning back against the sofa and closing his eyes. I slumped back, still next to him, but the distance between us felt huge.

Pulling on a hoodie, Cassius came to stand in front of me. With a gleam in his eye, he tugged the hood up over his head and put on a deep, sinister voice. "We're gathered here today to initiate you, Winter Huntington, into the cult of—"

"Cass? Shut the fuck up." Caiden rolled his eyes, and Cassius smirked at him, pulling his hood back down.

"Chill, mate. I'm just fucking around while we wait for Z. Where is he, anyway?" he muttered, as Weston entered the room, Kinslee following behind him. "West? Have you seen — Never mind." Zayde appeared in the doorway, holding a tray in his hands.

"What the fuck are you meant to be? The butler?" Cassius eyed him.

"Shut up, dickhead." Weston cuffed him round the back of the head.

"You're gonna pay for that."

I tuned out their bickering and watched as Zayde came closer, placing the tray on the coffee table.

Well.

I wasn't expecting that.

9

caiden

I smirked at Winter's sharp intake of breath as she stared at the tray, her eyes wide and confused. Zayde had given me a heads-up, so I knew what to expect, but I guess Winter hadn't seen what was in the bag that Creed had given to him.

Leaning forwards to take a closer look, my thigh brushed against Winter's again, and she shivered. Fuck, it was driving me crazy being so close to her and not being able to touch her. I wasn't going to deny myself anymore. Brushing her silky hair away from her face, I lined my lips up with her ear. "You okay there, Snowflake?" I murmured, trailing my hand down through her hair, down her back, and around her waist, pulling her closer to me. She sat statue still the whole time, but her shallow, quickened breathing gave her away.

"Y-yes," she managed to croak, her tongue darting out to lick her pouty lips. Fuck. I needed those lips wrapped around my cock. In fact, I needed to be buried inside her, fucking her until she was screaming my name. My dick stirred, hardening in my jeans, and I shuffled, trying to get myself under control.

Winter's head turned and her eyes darted down to my jeans, and she gave a gasp, her eyes widening even further. "Cade..." Her voice was tortured.

"It's what you do to me." I pulled her even closer so she was pressed right up against me, and she stared into my eyes. So many different emotions played across her face—I wondered what she was thinking.

She took a deep breath, and I could see the moment she came to a decision because a gleam came into her eyes, a wicked smile curving her lips. Leaning into me, she put her hand on my thigh, so fucking close to my cock that I had to bite back a groan. "You know what you need to do." Her voice in my ear was a sultry purr, her hand inching further up my thigh. "Let go, and trust me. That's all I'm asking for." Her lips brushed against my ear, her words taunting me. "Do you know what you do to me? Do you know how wet I am for you right now?"

Fucking hell.

I whipped my head around so fast that our lips brushed, before she could move. "You little cock tease," I growled, then before I knew it, my mouth was on hers, and she was kissing me back.

"No!" She pushed me away with an effort, both of us breathing heavily. "That wasn't fair. You don't get to kiss me yet."

I chuckled darkly. "What did you think was going to happen, when you were practically fondling my cock and heavy breathing in my ear?"

She pouted, a frown on her face, but I could see the smile she was trying to hide. Fuck, she was gorgeous. "Well. Just don't, okay?"

"Keep your hands to yourself, and we won't have a problem." I smirked at her as she huffed crossly, shrugging off my arm and slumping back again with her arms folded.

I suddenly became aware of everyone's eyes on us. I'd forgotten they were there, but they were all staring at us in amused silence.

"You two have issues," Zayde muttered, shaking his head.

"How the fuck could you get a boner when there's a severed finger staring at you?" Cassius' voice was incredulous.

"Fingers can't stare; they don't have eyes."

Cassius turned to my brother. "You know what I meant. Hey, maybe we could give this finger to Petr, to replace his missing one." He swiped the blood-encrusted severed finger from the tray, brandishing it in the air. "Hey, Littlefin—"

"Put. It. Down. Now." Zayde's voice was glacial, and Cassius dropped the finger back on the tray, pulling a face.

"Sorry, mate. Got a bit carried away."

My brother crossed to the tray and grabbed an antibacterial wipe from the packet there, throwing it to Cassius. "Use that."

Zayde pulled on a pair of latex gloves, snapping them into place.

"Bloody hell, Zayde in rubber gloves. I've seen it all now." Kinslee buried her face in Weston's shoulder, her laugh muffled.

Z ignored everyone, fully focused on his task. He gripped the finger and picked up a scalpel, scraping carefully at the decaying flesh around the ring that was still attached. It was so tight that the flesh was bulging either side of the metal band, so the only way to remove it was to cut it off. Me, I would've used pliers and pulled the thing off, but I guess Z didn't want to risk damaging it. Or maybe he just wanted to make the most of the opportunity to cut something. Hard to tell with him.

"That's fucking gross." Winter made a fake gagging sound but leaned closer to watch, fascinated. Zayde finished scraping away the flesh and worked the scalpel blade under the band of the ring, finally freeing it, and it fell onto the tray with a clatter.

He wiped the ring over with an antibacterial wipe, then began cleaning it using a cotton bud and jewellery cleaner.

"How do you have all this stuff?"

"Best not to ask," I murmured to Winter. She shuffled closer to me, and I forced myself to ignore the urge to touch her, focusing on Zayde's actions instead.

"Z. Can we get a fingerprint?" I indicated the severed digit.

He shook his head. "No prints. The boys said all his fingers were the same."

"That's fucking shady." I pulled on a pair of the latex gloves and picked up the finger, examining it more closely.

"Use the magnifying glass," Zayde suggested without looking up, still intent on cleaning up the ring.

"Can I see?"

I glanced up at Winter staring at the finger, curiosity in her blue eyes.

"C'mere, then." I tugged her onto my lap. She made a small noise of protest, but I held my arm around her waist like a steel band—she wasn't going anywhere. "Pick up the magnifying glass, and I'll hold the finger."

Obediently she took the magnifying glass from the tray, her hand shaking slightly. My girl was fighting her reaction to me—her little game of teasing me earlier had backfired, and she was back to being in denial about the way I affected her. I bit back a smug grin before she noticed; that would go down as well as a fucking lead balloon. "Good. Hold it over the top of the finger," I instructed.

I moved my face next to hers so we could both look through the glass. "See how the tip of the finger is all smooth?" I angled my head slightly, letting my stubble graze the soft skin of her cheek.

She shuddered, swallowing hard. "Yeah. How? How did it happen?"

"My guess," I said, moving my head again, my lips almost touching her skin, "is that they were burned off. It's a quick and easy way to do it. See how the skin's a different colour here?"

My stubble scraped against her cheek again as she nodded, but neither of us moved our faces away.

"Enough with the flirting, please," my brother groaned. "Sort your shit out. It's clear you both wanna be together. Fix whatever it is"—he glared at me—"*Caiden*, and we can all play happy families again."

"I'm kind of turned on watching the two of you," Cass interjected, waggling his eyebrows at us. Fucker.

Winter groaned, clearly uncomfortable, her cheeks flaming at the attention. "Please, Cass."

Best to ignore them.

I removed my arm from around Winter's waist. "Sit back down, Snowflake." She moved off my lap, leaning forwards and propping her chin on her elbows, which rested on her thighs. Before she had a chance to protest, I dropped a light kiss on her hair, then placed the severed finger down and quickly changed the subject. "Anyone else want to look at the finger?" No takers. "Z? You done with that ring yet?"

"Yeah." He indicated towards the magnifying glass, which Winter passed to him, and he studied the ring in silence for a moment, then wordlessly handed both the ring and the magnifying glass to me.

"Fuck," I breathed. "I think this is the same ring Petr was wearing that day at the hotel." It was a tarnished gold, sovereign-style ring. In the centre of the sovereign was a cloaked man with arms outstretched, one holding what looked like a lightning rod, and the other resting on top of what was either a number eight or an infinity symbol.

I passed both items to Winter, who studied them intently. "You're right. I'm sure of it. Do we have any photos of his hand wearing the ring?"

"Yeah, we do." I pulled my phone from my pocket and scrolled through my picture gallery as Winter passed the ring over to Cass. "Here." I zoomed in on the photo. It was clear that it was the same ring.

"This is great. I'm gonna send photos to Mercury and see what he can pull up." West stood, stretching. "Speaking of Mercury, he found something. It's not much, but it might be everything. He found record of Petr working at the docks last year. And, get this, he's also employed as a server at AMC. Right now. He's only had the position for a few months—looks like he works both there and at the Crown and Anchor. Dunno which days he works at AMC, but we need to check this out."

"This is great news." Winter smiled at Weston. "I finally feel like we're getting somewhere. Now we know there's most likely a connection between Petr and the dead guy. I mean, it's kind of clear to me at this point that the dead guy is the one who attacked me, since he was the one keeping me captive, and now he's dead, and whoever got me out of the docks took me to a hospital."

"I agree." Cass nodded. "Makes sense, and that was my feeling when we found the body. We have a probable connection between dead fingerless guy, Littlefinger, and the docks, so I'd say the odds are high."

"I'll send this stuff to Mercury now. Unless we need to discuss anything else?" West glanced at me, and I shook my head.

"I'm heading back to campus now." Kinslee stood.

"Do you have to go?" Winter pulled a sad face.

"Don't go guilt-tripping me, bitch. I've got shit to do." Kinslee gave Winter a stern look, and they both dissolved into laughter. Zayde raised a brow at me, and I shrugged, mouthing "women" to him.

"I'll drive you back. You wanna come?" Cassius turned to Winter, and she jumped to her feet.

"Yes, please. Can we stop at the shop on the way back? I've got a craving for Doritos, and you ate the last bag."

"Deal. As long as we can get chocolate."

"Goes without saying. Anyone else want anything?" Me and Z both shook our heads, and they left the room. We fell into silence as Zayde started packing away all his tools and whatever other shit he'd brought in.

"Z." I hadn't even meant to speak, but his sharp gaze shot to mine at my tone. *Fuck it.* May as well say what was on my mind. "I saw you and Winter earlier, when you got back from meeting Creed. You looked..." I trailed off, shrugging helplessly. "I don't know, comfortable with each other."

He remained silent, reading me as well as he always did, and I continued, asking him the one question I needed to hear the answer to. "Do you trust her?"

When he finally replied, after a long silence, he spoke the words simply, with no hesitation. "You know what? Yeah. I do."

"Why can't I have that with her?" I scrubbed my hand across my face, frustrated.

"You feel too much for her. Mate, I know you. You're not allowing yourself to trust her completely because it means opening yourself up to be hurt by her. You're trying to protect yourself."

Fuck. *Am I?* "I've fucked this up."

"No. Get your shit together, and let her in." He stood, holding the tray. "Just don't leave it too late." I saw an expression that could almost pass for sadness flicker in his eyes, gone before I could work out if it was really there or just my mind playing tricks on me. Then he was gone, and I was left alone with my thoughts.

Trust.

It went against everything I'd known. But then, the only people I *did* trust all trusted her. Maybe it was time to take that leap, and yeah, that was a scary as fuck thought, but the thought of Winter not being in my life? Or being with another man? Those were thoughts I wasn't even willing to entertain.

Time to man the fuck up and put myself on the line for my girl.

10

winter

My first day back at university, and I was itching for some normality. I'd managed to keep up with everything I'd missed, thanks to my lecturers sending me notes and assignments. In actual fact, we were so close to the end of the semester that the workload had eased right off. I only had one week left, and I'd be done until January.

After my morning lecture, I headed to the library, then met Cassius and Kinslee to get lunch.

As we entered the cafeteria, a hush descended on the room. People stopped talking. Literally stopped mid-conversation and turned to stare at me.

What the fuck?

Then the whispers started, growing in volume until they were too loud to ignore.

"I heard she gave James Granville a blowjob in the library."

"No, you're wrong. She had a threesome with James and his cousin. You know, the TA?"

"Yeah, he's hot. I'd have a threesome with them."

"What's so special about her, anyway?"

"Fucking slut, cheating on Caiden Cavendish."

"Who would even cheat on him?"

"I sucked his dick once. It was so big, I couldn't fit it all in. Made my jaw ache."

I gritted my teeth, straightening my spine.

Fuck them all and their rumours.

"Want to get out of here?" Kinslee whispered to me.

I shook my head. Better to face them, rather than run away like I was guilty.

Holding my head high, I continued making my way through the room to the lunch line. I chose and paid for my food on autopilot, answering Cassius and Kinslee without really hearing them.

As I slumped in my seat with a sigh, my skin prickled with awareness. I was so attuned to his presence that it felt like a magnet was pulling me in his direction.

I turned my head.

Over on the far side of the room was Caiden. My breath caught in my throat as I stared at him. His raven hair was all tousled, the muscles in his arms flexing under his tattoos as he leaned forward, planting one hand on the wall and shoving the other into the pocket of his jeans. He was so sexy, so assured, confidence radiating from him as he effortlessly commanded my attention, without even being aware he was doing so.

I wanted him.

So much.

It was taking everything I had to keep him in the friend zone, but I couldn't—

Wait a minute.

My eyes slid from Caiden to the person he was talking to. Until that moment, my entire focus had been on him, until I saw the slim hand landing on his arm, sliding up his bicep.

Hot, raging jealousy filled me, and I gasped aloud at the force of it. If I'd ever doubted my feelings for him, there was no doubting them now. My whole body vibrated with tension, desperate to race over to him and pry Portia's claws from his arm and claim him as mine.

Mine.

I couldn't tear my gaze away. I watched as he smiled down at her, watched her toss her perfect hair, batting her perfect eyelashes, thrusting her perfect tits towards him.

It hurt. Way, way more than I thought it would.

"Winter," Cassius hissed, bending his head to my ear and putting his arm around me. "All isn't as it seems."

"Isn't it?" I laughed bitterly. "Because from where I'm sitting, it looks like Portia's making a move on him, and he isn't doing anything to discourage her."

"That's your jealousy talking, babe. I shouldn't have to tell you, but he likes you. A lot. I knew it before either of you, and now he knows it, too." He gave me a smug smile. "There's no way he'd fuck things up. Plus, you asked him to trust you. That goes both ways."

"I know that," I mumbled. "It's her I don't trust. But what if he decides I'm not worth the effort?"

"You really think that?"

I made a non-committal noise, managing to finally tear my gaze away from Caiden, becoming aware that Cassius was still talking to me.

"Sorry, what was that? I zoned out for a minute."

He rolled his eyes but squeezed my shoulder reassuringly. "We're gonna sort out this shit with Granville. I've been thinking, and"—his voice dropped, so Kinslee and

I both had to lean in to hear him—"things aren't adding up. Have you got time to talk?"

I picked up my phone to check the time. "I've got a lecture in twenty minutes. I'll be free after that, though."

"Good. Meet me out the front of the Brunswick building at four o'clock. We need to go somewhere we won't be overheard."

"You're not leaving me behind." Kinslee's tone was firm, non-negotiable.

"Wouldn't dream of it, babe. I'll see if West is free, too. Z's...busy, and I don't wanna involve him or Cade yet, anyway. It might be speculation, but my instincts are never wrong."

"Never? You seem very sure of yourself." I laughed.

"Never."

"It's dark already." I shivered, pulling my beanie hat lower so it covered my ears, sinking down onto the large flat stone that Cassius had covered with a thick blanket from his car.

"Do we have to sit on this? Have you used it for, you know?" Kinslee shone her phone torch onto the wool hesitantly, then glanced over to Cassius, who was crouched over what the boys had told me was a fire pit.

"Have I fucked anyone on it, you mean?"

"Yeah."

"Yep." He grinned, looking far too pleased with himself.

"Ugh!" I jumped up, brushing off my jeans, as Kinslee pretended to vomit.

He rolled his eyes at us both. "You two have no sense of humour. Of course I haven't. West's sitting on that one."

"Cheers, Cass." Weston pulled a face.

"It's been washed, calm down."

"It better have."

Cassius shook his head and went back to building a fire. It was basically a small circular area in the courtyard of Alstone Castle, ringed with stones. Once he was finished, and he had a little fire going at the base of the pile, he leapt to his feet. "Chuck me the lighter fluid, will ya?" He pointed to a black plastic bottle near my feet, and I threw it to him. He sloshed a load of it over the logs.

"Burn, baby, burn!" he shouted, standing back and striking a match, throwing it into the midst of the pile.

There was a loud whoosh and a huge flame shot into the air, the sudden rush of heat making us all scramble backwards as quickly as we could.

"Fucking hell, Cass, how much lighter fluid did you put on that?" Weston stared at him in disbelief.

"Dunno." He shrugged, unconcerned, collapsing next to Weston on the large stone next to the one me and Kinslee were sitting on. We watched in silence as the flames licked greedily at the logs, burning through the lighter fluid and dying down to what I would call a "normal" fire. I basked in the warm glow, my numb face gradually regaining some feeling.

"Let's talk." Weston spoke softly. "Cass? You wanna tell us what you're thinking?"

Cassius nodded, then turned to look at me, his eyes glimmering in the firelight. "First, though. I need you to tell me what happened with Granville. And don't leave anything out."

I hadn't actually spoken to the Four about what had happened in any detail. I'd wanted to speak to Caiden, but when I'd realised he didn't trust me, there was no point. Kinslee was the only one who knew all the details.

Reliving the moment only served to make me angry all over again. I spoke through gritted teeth as I recalled James forcing his lips onto mine, then his vaguely threatening words to me: *"You and Cavendish deserve each other. I think I'm going to enjoy this, after all."* As I described how he'd left, bumping fists with Joseph, Joseph grasping a phone in his hand, a strange expression stole across Cassius' face.

"Fuck. No. No. No." He shook his head. "Why now?"

"Surely he wouldn't be that stupid, would he?" The worry was clear in Weston's voice, as he and Cassius exchanged glances.

"As if we didn't have enough shit to deal with. This is the fucking icing on the cake," Cassius growled.

"We're gonna have to tell Z."

"What if it sends him over the edge?"

"Fuck." Weston buried his face in his hands.

"Uh...would someone mind telling me what's going on?" I stared between them both, my heart racing, apprehension filling me.

They both turned to look at me, then silently communicating with their eyes, they both shook their heads.

"Listen, Winter." Cassius stood and came to sit down next to me. "It's not my secret to tell. We've had...run-ins with Joseph Hyde and his lemmings before. That's a big part of why we have so much security." He sighed heavily. "Granville may be a slimy fucker, but until now, he's stayed out of it."

"Mostly," Weston interjected with an eye roll.

"Yeah. Anyway, if they're starting shit again, we'll be ready." He slid his arm around me, gentling his voice. "I don't want you to worry about this, okay?" Peering around me, he met Kinslee's eyes. "That goes for you, too. We can handle it. Just...concentrate on getting to the bottom of, y'know, the stuff that we're already dealing with."

I frowned at Cassius. "Thanks for enlightening me. That literally tells me nothing. Can you at least tell me who or what I need to be watching out for?"

"Just stay away from Hyde and Granville, and anyone else related to them. You'll be fine. If this is what I think it is, they're not trying to hurt you. It's us they want to get to."

"If they're trying to hurt you, then they're hurting me," I said, a tremor in my voice. "You guys are my family, now. Please, just let me in. Maybe there's something I can do to help."

At my words, Weston rose from his seat and crossed to stand in front of me, pulling me up into his arms. He stroked his hands through my hair, the soothing motion reassuring me. "Winter. Trust us to handle this, okay? I promise you that if anything happens, we'll make sure you're not kept in the dark. We need to talk to Zayde and my brother first."

He kissed the top of my head and drew back so I could look into his eyes. His face was shadowed, but there was enough light from the fire that I could see his serious, imploring gaze. "Trust us?" He bit his lip, looking at me uncertainly. "Trust *me*? Please?"

My heart.

"West." I swallowed, speaking around the lump in my throat. "I trust you with my life." I raised my voice. "You too, Cass."

Cassius stood, tugging Kinslee up with him. "Good. We've got your back." His blue gaze turned to ice, and his voice hardened. "No one fucks with one of the Four, or our girls, and gets away with it. *No one*."

11

winter

I sang along with the radio as I whisked eggs for breakfast. I'd woken this morning feeling almost happy, weirdly, despite everything that was going on, even with the added James drama. After this week, the semester would be over. Kinslee's brother was coming home for the Christmas break, and we'd soon hopefully have some answers from him regarding the ship, the *Argo Navis*. Kinslee had decided it was better to wait until he was home and she could speak with him in person—he was working on an oil rig, with little to no communication, and no privacy in the small amount of contact he was able to have with the outside world.

The only blight in my day was the thought that soon I'd have to face my mother again. From what I'd learned from Weston, every year, the Alstone elite held a winter ball at Alstone Town Hall. I'd asked Kinslee for more details, but she hadn't been able to go before, nor had she had any desire to. She was at Alstone College thanks to a combination of her grandfather's money paying for her tuition and accommodation, and the small fact of her being the dean's goddaughter. Although she was what I'd probably call comfortably well off, until I came along, she'd stayed well away from the elite. Unfortunately for her, now, she was coming with me to the ball, slightly unwillingly.

Stupid archaic traditions dictated that we had to turn up in male-female couples—completely ridiculous in this day and age. I was going with Cassius, and since Caiden and I were still at a kind of impasse, he was taking Kinslee. I trusted both of them together, so of all the possibilities, them going as each other's date was by far the best option in my mind.

Anyway, that was a worry for another day. I crossed over to the fridge, pulling out the cheddar, and turned back around just in time to see Caiden saunter into the room, wearing a pair of black shorts, his torso glistening with sweat, rubbing his head with a towel.

My mouth went dry. Why was it that now we were in the friend zone, my body had decided to react even more strongly to his presence?

I placed the cheese carefully on the island and stood, just drinking him in.

"Hi." He lowered the towel and threw it around his neck, a smirk curving over his lips as he noticed me checking him out.

"Been working out?" I managed to say. Yeah, I asked the obvious question. I couldn't be expected to think, not when he was looking like that.

His smirk deepened. I gripped hard onto the edges of the island to stop myself from launching my body at his.

"Yeah." He prowled towards me, and I gulped as he stopped right in front of me. "You look sexy today," he murmured into my ear, then kissed my cheek and straightened up, carrying on to the cupboard where he proceeded to make himself a protein shake, never mind the fact that he'd left me helpless, longing for him.

"Cade. What's going on here?" I ventured. "Is this a game to you? Teasing me?"

He slammed his drink bottle down on the counter and was suddenly back in front of me before I had a chance to blink.

"What's going on is that I have some shit to work through. In the meantime, I'm reminding you of the facts so you don't forget them." Our gazes held, his stormy eyes darkening, reminding me more of thunderclouds at this point in time.

"What facts?" I licked my lips, my voice coming out hoarse.

He planted his hands on the island either side of me so I was trapped by his body, the heat and the sweat from his workout sending memories of nights spent together flashing through my mind like some kind of erotic film reel, making my thighs clench with need and my breath catch in my throat.

"Fact. You want me."

He leaned closer.

"Fact. I want you."

I shivered from both his words and his proximity.

"Fact. This one should come as a given, but don't think I didn't see the death stares you were giving to Portia yesterday. I'm not interested in anyone else."

"But she—" I began.

My words died away as he reached out and cupped my jaw, stroking his thumb over my pulse point. "No one compares to you, Snowflake. And that brings me on to my final fact. You'd better not forget this one."

"What is it?"

"You're. Fucking. *Mine*," he growled against my lips, then gave me a quick, hard kiss before I had a chance to even react to his words. He stalked away from me, swiping his drink bottle from the counter, and disappeared out of the kitchen.

I slumped back against the island on shaky legs, a smile spreading across my face.

Glad we were on the same page.

"Winter!" I spun around at the shout, seeing Weston jogging across the quad, and stopped, waiting for him, before I headed into the Student Union building with Kinslee.

"He's so hot," Kinslee muttered under her breath, her eyes raking over him as he drew closer. "I wish he wanted a repeat of our night together."

"Does he know you want a repeat?" I kept my voice low.

"Yes, but he's made it clear it won't happen." She clamped her mouth shut as he reached us, an easy grin on his lips, and I made a mental note to speak to her later. As far as I was aware, she wasn't seriously interested in him, but in her words, he was the best dick she'd ever had.

And that was a thought I didn't particularly want in my head, now he felt like my brother, and I knew he viewed me as a sister. Weird, really, since my relationship with Cade was almost the complete opposite.

I shook off my thoughts, realising Weston was speaking to me. "You ready for me to kick your ass at pool?"

"You think you can beat me?" I returned his grin.

"I'll catch up with you both later." Kinslee turned towards the cafeteria door.

Weston stopped her with a hand on her arm. "Do you have a minute? I need to talk to you both."

We both stared at him apprehensively. "Yes, I can spare a few minutes. What's up?"

"Come down to the bar." He let go of her arm, shoving his hands in the pockets of his slate-grey Alstone College hoodie and heading for the stairs leading down to the basement bar.

Once we were seated next to the pool table, he leaned forwards, resting his elbows on the metal table in front of us. He sighed. "It's about the winter ball. Kins, you can't go as Cade's date anymore. Dad's put his foot down, and he's arranged a date for Caiden. Some fucking shit about a huge business deal, and there's no way he can get out of it."

"What?" Kinslee and I exchanged glances.

"Yeah, I'm sorry. We both tried to talk him out of it, but he couldn't be swayed. Z's been dragged into it, too. Can't fuck up their deal." He deepened his voice, doing a scarily accurate impression of Arlo Cavendish. "This is our legacy, and your future. I'm depending on you to do the right thing."

"Don't worry about me." Kinslee leaned back in her chair. "I may not be one of the elite, but I can try to work something out, if you want me to be there."

"If you can, you know I'd love you there."

"I'll see what I can do. If I can't make it, you know the Four have your back." She nodded her head towards Weston, before standing up and swinging her bag onto her shoulder. "Don't stress. I've got to go now, otherwise I won't have time to eat before my next lecture."

We waved her off, and I turned back to West, asking him the question that I didn't want the answer to. "Who's Caiden's date? Please don't tell me it's Portia."

The grimace that appeared on his face told me I wasn't going to like his answer. "Jessa."

Jessa De Witt. Hot jealousy raged through me at the memory of her sneering, triumphant face, watching me as Cade fondled her tits, right before he pulled me off Cassius and dragged me upstairs and... The jealousy melted away as I remembered his heated kisses, the way he'd relentlessly fucked me, bringing me to the most powerful orgasm of my life...

"Winter? Are you okay?" My eyes snapped to Weston's, and I scrubbed my hand over my flushed face, trying to focus.

"I'm fine. I won't lie and say that the thought of Cade with her makes me want to poke out my own eyeballs so I don't have to see her, but I will suck it up and deal with it. I have no doubt that she'll try to rub it in my face every chance she gets, but I'm hoping Cade—" I groaned. "Who am I kidding? It's going to be fucking torture. Who's Zayde going with?"

"Portia."

I laughed. "I don't know if I feel more sorry for him, or for her. I bet neither of them wanted to go together, did they?"

"Doubt it. We'll stick together, anyway. It won't be all bad."

"I hope you're right."

"It's a masquerade ball. Maybe you could go for a full-on blindfold, then you won't have to look at the others."

"Ha. I might just do that."

He cocked his head at me. "If you're in agreement, me and Cass came up with an idea. You know the whole thing with James?"

I nodded. "What about it?"

"I know we said you should stay away from him and let us handle the situation, but we've been discussing it, and we're both in agreement. We thought that since you're not going to the ball with Cade, if you try and stay away from him the whole night, play up the fact you're not together, then that might get Granville to drop his guard. Since it looks like the whole purpose of that video was to drive you apart, if he thinks it's worked, it could be a good opportunity to get some information out of him."

"Hmm, that's not a bad idea, actually." I sat back, thinking. "So I'd be playing the angle of being grateful that I'm no longer with Cade since he's an irrational, jealous asshole, and see if I can get him to say anything that might give us an idea why the video even happened in the first place?"

"Exactly! I knew you'd understand." He grinned at me. "Cass won't let you out of his sight, so you don't need to worry about anything. Just see if you can get him to talk. To say anything at all."

"I can do that. Or attempt to, at least. You'd better give Caiden a heads-up, though. I don't want to actually make things any worse between us."

"Already on it," he assured me. He stood, scraping his chair back. "Come on. Let's get on with this game of pool. Loser has to cook dinner tonight, winner's choice of food."

"Deal." I blew him a kiss and leaned over the pool table, sending the white ball careening into the others, sinking two striped balls. "I'm in the mood for enchiladas tonight. Looks like you'll be busy in the kitchen."

"Cocky, aren't ya?"

I won the game. Just.

12

caiden

Speeding down the mostly empty road, one hand on the wheel, the other on the gearstick, I finally felt fucking free. This shit with Winter was messing with my head.

A Boogie Wit da Hoodie's "Swervin" melted the speakers, the thrumming beats echoing through the car as my phone started ringing. I hit the button to answer, turning down the stereo as I accelerated into a turn, feeling my R8 respond under me, the fucking sweet purr of the engine surrounding me and calming my mind.

Too bad it wouldn't last.

After the adrenaline rush of burning rubber, leaving dust in my wake as the unfortunate people in their average cars tried to keep up with me, I eased off on the accelerator and came to a halt outside my dad's mansion, waiting for the gates to open. Why did I get roped into this shit? Me and West had tossed a coin to see who would come here and pick up our suits that we'd had custom made for the ball, courtesy of my dad's tailor, but he'd guilt-tripped me so I didn't have a choice, whatever the coin had decided. To be fair, there wasn't much I wouldn't do for my younger brother, and if it meant making myself uncomfortable for half an hour or so, I'd do it, to save him the torture of being around Christine. I'd purposely timed my visit for early morning—if I was lucky, she'd still be in bed.

"What's up?"

My brother's voice came through the speaker. "Just wanted to remind you to pick up my Hydra cufflinks. I can't find them; I think they're still in my room, probably in the top drawer."

"Yeah, alright. I'll get them," I assured him, getting out of the car, holding my phone between my shoulder and my ear as I slammed the door behind me.

The front door was opened by one of my dad's security guys—I never knew their names, and he told me my dad was outside, training. Of course. He liked to stay fit, so he had a personal trainer come over first thing in the morning, three days a week.

I headed out through the kitchen and followed the path round to the stone terrace out the back of the house, where I found my dad with his personal trainer, doing cool-down stretches.

"Morning, Caiden," he greeted me, when he saw me standing there. Grabbing a towel, he rubbed it over his face, then handed it to his trainer. "You're early. Here to pick up your suits?"

"Yeah. Where—"

"One moment," he interrupted me, as his phone started blaring, vibrating across the stone wall it had been lying on. He strode over and swiped at the screen, talking to whoever it was in a low voice. I sank down on the wall to wait, while the trainer packed up the stuff he'd brought with him—

skipping ropes, resistance bands, and shit like that—putting it all inside a duffel bag. A movement in the corner of my vision caught my eye, and I glanced up to see Christine in a silk robe, gesturing at Allan, her face hard as she leaned forwards, shaking her head at him. I sighed aloud—guess I hadn't turned up early enough to miss her. Fingers crossed I could stay away from her, though—this early in the morning and she was already laying into the staff? Fuck going near her.

My dad snapped his fingers to get my attention and covered his phone with his hand as he turned to me. "This may take a while. Your suits are hanging in your room. See you all at the ball tonight, and behave, both of you."

I nodded, although he'd already dismissed me, returning his attention to his phone. Whatever. Now Christine was up, I wanted to get out of here as quickly as possible. I managed to get upstairs, retrieve our suits and West's cufflinks, and make it out of the front door without her seeing me.

Thank fuck for that.

Walking into the kitchen, I was greeted, or more like assaulted, by a sight that it was way too fucking early to see. Cassius, naked as the day he was born other than a black apron that said "Warning: Concealed Sausage" on it, switching between grilling bacon and having what sounded like another code name discussion with my brother and Winter.

I groaned, loudly, and all three of them turned to look at me. "Cass? Why the fuck are you naked?"

He shrugged. "Why not?"

Okay then. I shook my head at him, crossing to the island. Sometimes with Cass, it was best not to ask.

"Did you get my cufflinks?" West eyed me hopefully, and I nodded.

"What cufflink—ow, fuck!"

I looked round just in time to see Cassius jump a mile in the air, gripping his ass, his expression pained.

"The fucking bacon fat jumped out of the pan and burned me!"

"Wouldn't have happened if you didn't have your ass out. Just saying." I shrugged.

"Aww, Cass. You want me to kiss it better?" Winter smirked, and my amusement died away. I glared at them both, and Winter mouthed *joking*.

Not funny. It was too early for this shit.

Zayde walked in, took one look at Cass, turned around, and walked straight back out again, making Cass and Weston collapse in fits of laughter, the burn forgotten. Weston picked up a spatula, and shouted "en garde," to Cassius, and they started fucking around, having a pretend sword fight with the utensils.

Rolling my eyes, I pulled out my phone, letting them get on with it. I caught Winter's eye, and she gave me a tiny, hesitant smile, which I returned straight away, making her eyes sparkle as she just looked at me. She was so fucking gorgeous, even when she was sleepy and trying to wind me up.

Playing around apparently finished, Cassius dropped his wooden spoon, staring between us, as Winter yawned widely. A gleam came into his eye. "Hey, Winter. You seem like you're tired. You know what you need?"

Her voice was flat and unamused as she took in his expression. "What."

"Vitamin D. From Cade."

For fuck's sake.

"Vitamin D? What?" She raised a brow at him, and he gestured to his crotch.

"Ladies love the vitamin D."

"Really." She shook her head, caught between an eye roll and a smile. "Is that bacon done yet? I need food to keep my strength up. Got to be ready for the ball."

The ball. Yeah, that was going to be a shitshow. Being forced to go with Jessa was torture enough, and seeing Winter there—okay, she was going to be with my mate—but that didn't mean it would be any easier. Especially since we weren't together at the moment.

Which reminded me, better leave everyone with a reminder that even though we weren't together, she was mine.

I slid off my stool and walked around behind her. She kept facing forwards, still talking to Cassius, but her breathing sped up, and I saw goosebumps spread over her arms as I pressed my body up against hers, brushing her hair off her shoulder. Fuck, she felt so fucking good against me. I needed to get my shit together and get my girl back.

Leaning down, I spoke into her ear, keeping my voice low. "Jessa may be my date tonight, but that's as far as it goes. You're the only one I want." I had to grip the marble island on either side of her, crowding her in, to stop myself from touching her, doing something I shouldn't, like picking her up and carrying her out of the kitchen and fucking her until she couldn't see straight.

She made a tiny noise in the back of her throat. "I...oh. *Cade.*"

My name coming from her lips? Best fucking sound ever. I glanced up at the boys to see them both watching me, and then I kissed her cheek and stepped back, giving her space to breathe.

Hopefully, all three of them got the message.

She was mine.

13

winter

This whole situation was fucked up. For a start, the date situation. But even worse than that? Yes, it got worse. My mother had decided to brush our little disagreement in the coffee lounge aside and pretend it had never happened, and she'd invited me to get ready at her mansion. Actually, "invited" wasn't really the word I'd use, more "insisted." I'd been tempted to refuse, but I didn't want to rock the boat with this night being important to so many influential people—including the Four, thanks to this huge business deal that was currently being negotiated. I wasn't aware of any of the details, but if it all went to plan, it would allow Alstone Holdings to expand internationally and create more employment opportunities.

So that was why I was currently standing in the bedroom I'd been allocated in the Cavendish home, being scrutinised by Renée, the stylist hired by my mother to prepare me. Clearly, she wasn't taking any chances with me choosing anything inappropriate. Somewhere in the house, she was being attended to by a whole team of people, but thankfully she'd deemed that one person was enough for me.

"I have a few different dresses that could work," Renée mused, tapping her lip in thought. Reaching into the bag at her waist, she pulled out a phone. "Allan, please could you have the garment bags numbered four, seven, and sixteen brought up to Miss Huntington's room? Thank you." Replacing the phone, she turned to me. "Please could you remove your clothing, other than your underwear?"

"Um. Okay." I padded into the bathroom and stripped off, pulling on a robe over my underwear. By the time I'd finished and re-entered the bedroom, there were three garment bags laid across the bed.

"Let's try the first outfit." Renée carefully unzipped one of the bags, revealing a long, shimmering grey dress. I shrugged out of my robe, and she helped me into the dress, smoothing the silky material down, then stepping back to run a critical eye over me. "Turn around, please."

I obediently spun around, and she pursed her lips. "I don't think this one is quite right for you. Let's move on to the next one."

As she unzipped the next bag, withdrawing a bundle of black tulle, my heart started beating faster. The fabric slid over my body, slipping into place effortlessly.

Renée clapped her hand over her mouth, her eyes shining, and she pointed towards the mirror.

"Oh." I stared at my reflection. Was this really me? "This dress is perfect," I whispered, as Renée came to stand next to me, fluffing out the skirt.

"Perfect for you. Not everyone can pull off the black, but for you? It works beautifully." She smiled. "No need to try the other dress. This is the one."

I nodded in agreement, still staring. The dress was a

black, floor-length ball gown. The bodice was sheer lace overlaid with black applique embellishments which covered my breasts and connected with the skirt, with tiny gems interlaid in the fabric. The skirt itself was made of layers of tulle, flowing down from my waist and skimming the floor, with a small train at the back.

"With the hair and make-up, and the mask, you'll be a vision. Hurry, we don't have long."

The doorman gave a small bow as I passed between the huge stone columns and entered Alstone Town Hall. My mother and Arlo had headed inside already, but I'd taken a moment to compose myself, needing to prepare to face what waited for me inside. Namely Caiden, with Jessa. There was no doubt that she'd be all over him, and no matter what, I couldn't make a scene or let her know how she affected me.

I glanced at myself in the large mirror that hung in the entrance foyer, adjusting my mask. My hair had been curled, falling in waves down my back, and underneath the crystal-studded black lace mask I wore, my eyes were rimmed in smoky shadow. My lips were slicked with a simple, natural lip colour, and my skin had been lightly dusted with a shimmery powder. I wore no jewellery, the mask and the dress making enough of a statement on their own.

Taking a deep breath, I walked down the corridor to the doors that would lead me into the ballroom.

"Would you like to wait for your escort, madam?" I turned, my hand already reaching out for the door, to see a uniformed man eyeing me, a polite smile on his face.

"Um. I'm meeting him inside." I'd sent Cassius a

message just before we'd left the car, then strapped my phone to my thigh with the ingenious garter purse Renée had given me. Earlier, he'd sent me a photo of the mask he was going to be wearing—black, metallic, Roman warrior style, with gold embellishments showing two Pegasus horses, and a skull with crystal eyes in the centre. All of the Four, in fact, would wear the same masks, but I knew I wouldn't have any trouble spotting them, regardless.

The uniformed man nodded, opening the door with a gloved hand.

I stepped inside.

I was standing at the top of a huge, sweeping staircase, descending down to the darkened ballroom below, illuminated by soft spotlights that bathed the room in shades of blue and purple. Balconies ran down each wall, held up by tall marble columns. Huge crystal chandeliers hung from the vaulted ceiling, which was decorated in gold leaf. A large stage stood at the far end of the ballroom, where what looked like a full-on orchestra played. Groups of people decked out in beautiful gowns, tuxedos, and all kinds of masks filled the entire room, talking, dancing, and drinking.

Faking a confidence I most definitely didn't feel, I straightened my shoulders, held my head high, and carefully descended the staircase, holding the tulle skirt of my dress so I didn't trip.

At the bottom of the stairs, from behind a Roman warrior mask, a pair of stormy ocean eyes arrowed straight to mine. His jaw fell open, and then he closed it, swallowing hard. No one else existed in that moment.

"Winter." His voice caressed my ears. "You look... You're so fucking beautiful."

I stepped towards him, my heart pounding as I took in his darkened gaze, his body filling out his dark suit so deliciously, his hair styled to perfection.

"Caiden," I whispered. I needed his touch.

"We can't," he said hoarsely, as I reached him.

"I know." There was a lump in my throat. I felt a hand on my arm, and then Cassius was steering me away.

"That was quite an entrance, babe. Good thing Jessa and Portia weren't there to witness Cade's reaction to you. I've never seen him look like that before. Ever."

"What reaction?" My heart fluttered.

"He looked at you like you're his world."

I couldn't reply.

I just let him lead me deeper into the crowd, away from the one person I wanted to be with, but couldn't be.

"Listen. I know it's hard, yeah? But remember our goal. Make Granville think you're not interested in Caiden, try and get him to drop his guard so we can get some answers. And try not to kill Jessa."

I gritted my teeth. "Where is she, anyway?"

"I dunno, she had to go with Portia to the bathroom or some shit. Come on, let's get a drink, then we'll see if we can spot Granville. All these bloody masks make it ten times harder, but thanks to my skills, I found out he's wearing this one." He pulled his phone from his pocket and showed me an image from James' social media account, posted earlier, showing him with his arm around a brunette in a red dress (from what I could see of it, anyway) who was blowing a kiss at the camera, both of them wearing gold Venetian-style masks.

"Okay, let's do this." I scanned the crowds as we walked,

taking the glass of champagne Cassius grabbed from a passing waiter. "Shall we dance once we've finished our drinks? The dance floor is a bit clearer—we might be able to see better."

"Yeah, good idea."

On the dance floor, I let Cassius tug me closer. "Cade was right. You do look beautiful. He's a lucky fucker." He paused. "Or he will be, when he gets his shit together." His eyes travelled down my body. "Your tits look fucking phenomenal in that dress. Just saying."

"Cass, please," I groaned, but I couldn't help the smile that crossed my lips. I shook my head at him. "As much as I should comment on what you just said... Never change."

He grinned widely, giving me a wink from behind his mask, and we moved across the dance floor in time to the music.

"Winter!" I spun in Cassius' arms at the sound of Weston's voice, and then I was in his arms. He kissed my cheek, then drew back to look at me. "Wow. Has Cade seen you, yet?"

I nodded, my mouth twisting.

"Sorry, sis. I know it's hard to be here. If it's any consolation, it's just as hard for him. Y'know?"

"I know. I just hate it. I wish we were together. I haven't even seen him with Jessa yet."

"That girl has got nothing on you." A quiet but firm voice came from near my ear, and I glanced away from Weston to see Lena standing next to him. Unlike the last (and only) time I'd seen her, she didn't have a sulky pout on her face. Her blonde hair was curled, like mine, and although she still had masses of black eyeliner rimming her eyes, with her black, feathered mask, the whole effect was striking. She had on a long, black, off-the-shoulder floor-length prom dress, fairly modest and not what I would have expected, going by the last time I'd seen her.

She must've read my thoughts, because she sighed and rolled her eyes, gesturing at herself with black-painted nails. "My mother picked out this dress. I got to choose the colour, and the mask, but that was it."

"Oh. I wasn't judging, by the way." I cleared my throat and met her eyes. "To be honest, I was thinking that it didn't seem like something you'd pick. Not that I know you. In fact, I don't think we were ever properly introduced."

"You're right. I wouldn't have picked this." She gave me a wry smile. "I'm Lena. Aka the moody bitch, according to my brother."

Cassius laughed. "Not wrong, though, am I?"

"Cass." Weston frowned at him. Or at least, I think he did. It was hard to tell with the mask he was wearing.

"I'm Winter." I jumped in before Cassius could make the situation any worse.

"I know. Love your tatts by the way. I wanted to tell you at the other party, but I wasn't in the best mood. No offence, but your mother's parties are boring as fuck. I'd have more fun at a funeral."

A surprised laugh burst out of me. "You and me both." I turned to Cassius. "Why don't you invite Lena over sometime?"

He pulled a face. "Why would I want my annoying sister hanging around?"

I punched him in the arm.

"I like her." Lena grinned at him.

"Fuck me, Lena's proper smiling. It's a miracle." Cassius staggered backwards with an exaggerated gasp.

"You wanna dance? Or get a drink?" Weston murmured to her, shooting Cassius a glare.

“Can we get some air?” She looked up at him, and his gaze softened as he turned away from Cassius and met her eyes.

“Course. Come on.” He slid his arm around her, and I watched as he manoeuvred them away through the crowds, using his strong body to protect her from being jostled.

Next to me, Cassius gave a heavy sigh.

“What’s wrong?”

He shook his head, muttering, “It doesn’t matter.”

“Cass. Talk to me.” I put my hand on his arm.

“Nothing. I don’t like seeing them together, that’s all.”

“West and Lena?”

“Yeah. I know our dads forced them to come here together, but I’m not blind. I know West’s got a bit of a thing for her, even though he denies it. It would be a fucking disaster if anything happened between them. My best mate and my sister? No fucking way.”

I stared at him, deep in thought. “Are you sure he’s interested? She’s still at school, isn’t she? I thought he liked older women.”

He shook his head. “Yeah, she’s still at school, but she’s eighteen now, as of last week. Not that it matters, West likes women, generally. He doesn’t care if they’re older or not.”

“Do you think she’s interested in him, though? And is he really into her? I don’t think he’s any different with her than he is with other girls.”

“He’s...I dunno, protective of her.” He shrugged.

“He’s protective of me, too,” I pointed out.

“Yeah, that’s true. Maybe I’m paranoid. I just don’t want anything getting fucked up, and me having to choose between them or something.”

I stepped closer to him, putting my arms around him, unable to bear his downcast expression. “Hey. You’re worrying about nothing. West likes having fun with girls, he doesn't get serious about them. A bit like someone else I know—" I did a fake cough. "—you." And he laughed. "I'm positive he wouldn't do that to Lena. Your friendship with him is far too important."

"Look at you, being all wise and shit." He kissed my cheek, his expression brightening. "Thanks, babe. I appreciate it. You wanna dance some more?"

"Why not?"

During a lull in the music, I was catching my breath after being dragged all over the dance floor by Cassius, both of us hoping to spot James, when something, or should I say, someone caught my eye.

"Cass!" I hissed. "Don't look, but is that...? Is that the prime minister? No, it can't be."

He followed my gaze, then nodded slowly. "Hard to tell with the mask, but I think so, yeah. Look over there at the security, trying to be all discreet and blend into the background."

"Wow."

"Alstone elite, baby. These people are connected."

"I'm starting to see that," I murmured.

"Oh, fuck," Cassius mumbled under his breath, staring over my head, and the prime minister was forgotten as I spun around to see Caiden. With Jessa.

14

winter

There was no denying how good they looked together. Jessa's long dark hair shone under the spotlights, and her slinky jade-green dress clung to her body. A matching jade mask, feathered and embellished with crystals, sparkled as they moved to the music.

I'd been expecting the hot jealousy that burned through me at the sight of them, but it still hurt, and I gripped Cassius harder, making him hiss. "Winter."

"Shit, sorry, Cass." I loosened my grip where my nails had been digging into his arms.

He pulled me closer, speaking into my ear. "Are you ready? You know when she sees you, she's gonna want to rub it in your face?"

"Yeah, I know." I gritted my teeth.

"Look at him. He's not enjoying it, babe." His tone became lighter, amused, as he twisted us round, then spun me back to face them. "Look at Z."

I became aware of Zayde with Portia, stunning in a deep blue ball gown. He, like Cade, was dressed all in black. Black suit, black shirt, black tie. His mouth was set in a grim line, his body stiff, holding Portia as far away from him as he could. To be fair, she didn't look any happier to be with him. I smirked, before my eyes returned to Caiden.

I noticed the exact moment he saw me. He grimaced, and Jessa looked up at him, and then her head shot round towards me. She deliberately stepped closer to Cade, clinging onto him, running her hand up his arm, a satisfied smile on her lips as she watched me shoot daggers at her with my eyes. Caiden's jaw tightened, but he let her touch him, playing his part, just as I was.

I *hated* it.

Cass spun me away, before I could do anything stupid like launch myself at her. What was it about Caiden Cavendish that made me so fucking jealous of any woman that was around him?

Like a magnet, my eyes kept going straight to his, catching glimpses of him across the dance floor, and every time, he was looking right back at me.

"James. To your left," Cassius suddenly hissed in my ear. "Act like Caiden is invisible to you. I'm moving us closer." He skilfully twisted us between dancing couples, until I lost sight of Caiden and we were next to James and his date. I steeled myself, wishing Kinslee was here as backup. Despite her assurances, she hadn't been able to get a date at such short notice, and with the ball being so exclusive, we couldn't work anything out.

Mentally shaking my head, I prepared myself.

"James." I pasted a small, hesitant smile on my face, not too wide, in case he got suspicious. "Could I have a quick word with you?"

His eyes were shadowed behind his gold mask, so I couldn't make out his expression, but I heard his sharp, surprised intake of breath. He glanced between me and his date, who was staring at me intently, before her eyes were drawn to Cassius.

"Hi, Cassius," she murmured softly, and then her focus returned to me. "I don't believe we've been introduced. I'm Bea."

"Winter." I smiled at her, not sensing any hostility, and she returned my smile.

"Bea, how have you been? Haven't seen you for ages." Cassius took control of the situation, nudging me as he moved in front of Bea, and I took the chance to lean into James.

"Please? Just a quick word?"

He looked back at his date, who gave a small nod before returning her attention to Cassius and followed me from the dance floor. I needed to go somewhere I could talk to him without being overheard, but at the same time, I needed to be within eyesight of Cassius. For lack of other options, I headed towards the back of the room, rounding one of the marble columns to give us a small amount of privacy.

"We need to talk, don't you think?"

He glanced around us, then nodded slowly, moving deeper into the shadows and leaning against the wall. I could see Cassius and Bea out of the corner of my eye, not close enough to overhear our conversation, but close enough for Cass to watch out for me.

"Listen, I've actually been debating whether to get in contact with you, but I wasn't sure how you'd react." His shoulders slumped, and he sighed heavily. "I wanted to apologise to you for what happened in the library."

"Why do it, though? I thought we were friends."

Scuffing his foot against the floor, he hesitated for a

moment, dropping his gaze to the floor. "I didn't have a choice."

"What's that supposed to mean?" All thoughts of my plan to pretend to be grateful to him for driving a wedge between me and Caiden went out of the window at the undercurrent of fear in his tone. When he didn't answer, I moved even closer, placing a hand lightly on his arm. "James?"

He spoke low and quickly. "When I kissed you, I was feeling pissed off—I'd heard about Cavendish's little display claiming you in the cafeteria, and it made me...I don't know, jealous, in a way, I guess. He's never been interested enough in any girl before to do anything like that, and it had to be the one that I had first, the one I'd been friends with. It didn't take much persuading to kiss you, and when you reacted so angrily, it made me angry in turn, and at that point I was glad I'd done it."

My head was spinning, as I tried to process what he was telling me. "Okay. I understand all that, I suppose, not that I agree with your reasons. At all. But why, James? Why didn't you have a choice? Who's behind all this?"

"I can't tell you. I wish I could stay out of it, and I'm sorry you got caught up in everything."

That told me nothing. I needed answers. "Joseph's involved, though, right?"

He stiffened at the mention of his cousin. "You're a nice girl, Winter. But you being here, being related to the Cavendish family..." He sighed. "Whether you wanted to or not, you've chosen your side. You wouldn't be willing to go against your family, would you?"

"What do you mean by 'side'?" I tried to keep the impatience from my voice, so fed up with all this secrecy.

Why couldn't anyone speak like normal people, instead of being all cryptic and shit?

"I'm telling you this because I like you, and you've been nothing but nice to me, and despite what you might think of me right now, I'm not the bad guy here."

Beckoning me closer, he bent down to speak into my ear, and I held my breath. "Understand this. Alstone has rivalries dating back for generations, in some cases. When you first turned up, I honestly didn't know who you were. If I had, I would've kept my distance. To begin with, it seemed okay—the Four clearly didn't want you around, and I thought that you and I could be friends. When it became obvious that Cavendish had a thing for you, and especially after he threatened me, I backed right off."

His voice lowered even further. "My cousin's family, and my family, to a lesser extent, are bitter rivals with all the founding members of Alstone Holdings. Sometimes, you have to do things for your family that you may not want to do, because they're your blood."

Drawing back, I peered at him, trying to see his eyes behind his mask. "I get that, but no. You don't have to. If it goes against your beliefs and morals, you say no. And you know what?" I waved my arm in the direction of the dance floor. "Those four boys? They're *my* family. Yeah, we're not related by blood, but the fact remains that we're a family. And while I'd do almost anything for them, I wouldn't blindly follow orders that went against my instincts, and not only that, I know they'd never ask me to compromise my beliefs or standards."

He shook his head. "Count yourself lucky, then, but you wouldn't be saying that if you were in my position." Straightening up and moving away from the wall, he stared at me again. "That's all I can tell you. I'm sorry, but I want to stay out of it as much as possible. Just...try and do the same, okay? Stay away from trouble."

I couldn't help laughing, a low, bitter laugh. "Trouble seems to follow me around, ever since I came to Alstone."

"Be careful. Goodbye, Winter." With that warning lingering in the air, he strode away, beckoning to Bea, who returned to his side, and they were swallowed by the crowd.

Cassius was in front of me in an instant, and I gave him a rundown of the situation.

"As I thought," he muttered. "Another fucking complication we could do without."

"Do you think there could be any connection between this shit with James and Joseph, and my mother?" I voiced the question that had been bugging me since the boys had alluded to past issues with them.

Cassius paused for a moment, thinking, then shook his head slowly. "No. there's no way. It wouldn't make any sense."

"Okay." He was right. It didn't make sense, not really. I was just grasping at straws, sick of not having any answers.

"Come on. I've had enough dancing for one night." Taking my hand, he led me towards the doors at the back of the room.

I was halted by a manicured hand on my arm. "Winter. Come and dance with your stepfather."

I stared at my mother. "Sorry, what?"

She huffed, pursing her red-painted lips. With her delicate silver mask, her mermaid-style silver gown covered in hundreds of tiny crystals, and her dark hair, so similar to mine, falling down her back in soft waves, she was stunning. "Come and dance with Arlo." Stepping closer to me, she lowered her voice. "Remember what we spoke about on the way here."

Right.

She turned to me, the privacy partition up so the driver wouldn't overhear our conversation. "Winter. Tonight is important for us, and for Alstone Holdings. There's been some...gossip regarding your little incident at the Wilson Lounge. You know how people are. I've managed to smooth things over, for the most part, by explaining that you've been having a difficult time adjusting to living here, and you're having trouble dealing with the loss of your father."

I sat silently, my teeth gritted, my nails digging into my palms. I didn't trust myself to speak.

"Winter," Arlo cut in, a slight frown on his face. "As you're well aware, I'm in the process of negotiating this business deal, and it's important that we present a united front. This deal is worth a huge amount of money, not to mention the additional employment opportunities it will create." He leaned forwards. "Your mother and I aren't asking for much. Be polite, be seen interacting with us during the evening, preferably somewhere prominent. Can you do that for me?"

"Yes." Despite my relationship with my mother, I wasn't about to purposely try to ruin things for Arlo. Especially since he wasn't the only one who'd be affected.

"Good girl." He leaned back in his seat, dismissing me, and my mother smiled at me, a smile that didn't reach her eyes.

"Caiden seemed more than happy to be taking Miss De Witt to the ball as his date. Lovely young lady, isn't she? Very pretty."

"Lovely," I gritted out, picking up my phone and making a point of unlocking the screen and scrolling to my messages. This conversation was over.

. . .

At the sound of a throat clearing I came back to the present to see Arlo holding out his hand, a brow raised expectantly. "Shall we?"

Nodding once, I placed my hand in his.

"Christine, you're a vision of loveliness." Cassius laid on the charm, and my mother lapped it up. Their conversation faded away as Arlo led me back to the dance floor and placed one hand on my waist, keeping a respectable distance between us as he spun us between the dancing couples. He didn't try to speak to me, either, which I was grateful for.

Our dance was interrupted by a man dressed in a black suit with an earpiece, who tapped Arlo on the shoulder.

"Sir? We have a situation."

"Excuse me, Winter." Arlo nodded to me, then strode away, and I stared after him, debating. It could be nothing, but I wanted to follow him. I made my way off the dance floor in the direction Arlo had gone, passing my mother, who was dancing with an older man with white hair. I vaguely recognised him from the party at her house. Cassius was deep in conversation with a man and woman, so I decided to take my chance while he was occupied. I knew I shouldn't disappear on my own, but really, what was the harm? I mouthed *bathroom* to him as I passed on my way to the back of the ballroom, and he gave me a half nod before returning to his conversation.

Stepping outside the doors, I headed down a corridor at a fast walk, keeping an eye out for Arlo. I caught a glimpse of a suited figure turning into a room up ahead and slowed my pace, not wanting him to be aware of my presence.

Reaching the room, I bent down, pretending to adjust my shoe, listening intently to the conversation I could hear snatches of through the partially open doorway.

"Who? ... told you to take care of it ... docks ... I don't have time for this ... That's what I pay you for ... be discreet."

The door was suddenly thrown open and Arlo stormed out, in the opposite direction to me, to my relief. I don't know what he'd have done if he'd caught me right outside the door, but I didn't want to find out. I straightened up and continued down the hallway, discreetly peering into the room as I passed. All I could see was the security guy who had come to get Arlo on the dance floor, and the back of a man's head, with a small round bald patch in his greying hair. Something about him felt familiar, but I couldn't put my finger on it.

As I walked by at a snail's pace, I saw the security guy mutter something to the other man, so low and quiet that I couldn't catch his words. He gestured angrily, throwing his hands up, before following Arlo out of the room.

I made a mental note to think about it later and followed the signs to the bathrooms. There wasn't anything else I could do right now—the last thing I wanted was to get caught, unable to explain myself. Being Arlo's stepdaughter, I wasn't exactly able to fly under the radar.

My head was swimming, though. I could've sworn Arlo had mentioned the docks. It could be a coincidence—after all, they were owned by Alstone Holdings. But I couldn't ignore the feeling I had that something more was going on.

Lost in my thoughts, I was washing my hands in the ornate marble bathroom when the door swung open, and Jessa and Portia stepped inside. I groaned under my breath, steeling myself.

"Having fun, Winter?" Portia smirked at me, coming to stand in front of the mirrors, pulling a blood-red lipstick from her purse. "How does it feel, knowing Caiden ditched you for someone who's actually in his league?"

Jessa met my eyes in the mirror, flicking her long hair back with a triumphant smile. “You did me a favour, babe. He’s been all over me tonight. I can’t wait for the after-party.”

“Private party for two,” Portia sang, before pouting in the mirror, slicking her lipstick on, then smacking her lips together.

“You know it.” Jessa pulled her own lipstick out of her purse, deliberately holding eye contact with me. “With my father negotiating this deal with his father, I just know we’re going to be spending much more time together. To grow a lot closer, if you know what I mean.”

Portia dug a small brush out of her clutch bag, running it through her silky hair. “You know him intimately already, babe. And he’s been back for seconds.”

“And thirds.”

“And why wouldn’t he? You’re perfectly suited. Everyone keeps saying how good you look together tonight.” She turned to me, her tone conversational. Throughout their whole exchange I’d been kind of frozen in place, desperate to be anywhere else, but at the same time wanting to hear what they had to say. I needed to leave. “Did you know I’ve been with Caiden, too? Most of our friends have. You’re nothing special.” Tucking her brush back into her bag, she fluffed out her hair as Jessa pouted at her reflection. “Him and Jessa are going places.”

I rolled my eyes. Yeah, I was so fucking jealous at the thought of Jessa with Cade that it made me feel sick, but I wouldn’t let them get to me. At least, I’d try. Actually putting that thought into action was way, way harder when I had them both filling my ears with their poisoned words. “You two are so deluded,” I managed to spit out, miraculously without my voice cracking, spinning on my heel, and racing out of the bathroom to the sound of their laughter.

"Winter." Stopping at the voice, temporarily distracted, I turned to see Zayde leaning against the wall.

"Z? What are you doing here?"

"Waiting for my date." His lip curled. "Can't fucking wait to get out of here and ditch her."

"Not a fan of Portia, huh? Me neither." Understatement of the evening.

He pulled his phone from his pocket, his tone turning icy. "You could say that." Eyes on his phone, he inclined his head to the left and added, "You might want to go that way."

Okay then.

I was in no rush to get back to the ballroom, and I was more than happy to put as much space between me, Portia, and Jessa as possible, so I followed his vague instruction, continuing down the corridor. I passed a set of glass double doors that were thrown open, allowing a cool breeze to blow in, and paused, taking in the unexpected view. There was a garden through the doors, all manicured hedges with lights artfully placed throughout the space, and at the bottom stood a small bandstand draped in white fairy lights.

I took a step forwards to explore, when I was pulled back against a hard body, arms coming around my waist, holding me in place.

He rasped one word against my ear.

"Snowflake."

15

caiden

"You know I'm gonna have to punish you for what you did." I advanced on Granville, stalking him like a lion would with its prey, taking my time, toying with him, knowing he wasn't going anywhere. I shouldn't be doing anything to potentially fuck things up for the Alstone Holdings deal, but we were in private, and I knew he wouldn't say anything. This had been coming ever since he tried to trick Winter, and from what I could see of his face, he was resigned to his fate.

He swallowed hard, his voice shaking. "I know. I didn't have a choice, though."

"Don't give a shit." I spat the words. "You fucked around with me and her, and you have to pay."

"Just—just make it quick, okay? Don't get blood on my suit. It's a Boateng." He gave me a pleading look from behind his mask, but I was too angry to pay it any attention. Discarding my suit jacket by the bathroom door, which I'd locked, I advanced on him, undoing my cufflinks and rolling up my sleeves.

Crack.

My well-placed punch to his jaw sent his head swinging round, and he was on the floor before I knew it. Fucking pussy. "Get up."

He gasped, scrambling into a sitting position, his mask askew. "Please. Don't do this. Winter wouldn't like it."

His words gave me fucking pause, piercing through my rage. What would she think? I stared down at him on the floor, torn between my need to exact revenge, and the knowledge that he was most likely right.

For fuck's sake.

I kicked out at the wall next to his head, hard, sending a shower of plaster raining down on the floor and making him flinch, then stalked towards the door, swiping my jacket from the floor, and leaving him cowering behind me.

"Cade?" Winter's voice was hesitant.

I blinked, coming back to the present and the girl I had in my arms.

Seeing her tonight? I'd been fucking speechless. It wasn't even the dress—it was *her*. Everything had slammed into place, and all I wanted was to go to her, to let everyone know she was mine. It had been torture keeping my distance and having to entertain Jessa. After I'd confronted Granville, I'd talked Z into taking her and Portia back to our place for the after-party we'd planned, right before I saw Winter slipping out of the ballroom, and I owed him, big time. I'd made it clear to Cass that I'd be coming after Winter and he could leave. The ball would be over soon enough; as far as I was concerned, I'd done my duty, and now my only concern was my girl.

Keeping my arms around her, I walked us out of the doors and over to the side of the building. I spun her in my arms, then let go, reaching up to undo my mask. She did the same, her hands trembling, and I took her mask, placing it with mine on the stone ledge next to us.

"Shouldn't you be with Jessa?" Her mouth turned downwards, and all I wanted to do was kiss her pouty lips and make her smile again, but I had things I needed to say.

I crowded her up against the wall, leaning in and running my nose up her jaw to her ear. I ignored her question and instead asked one of my own.

"Guess what?"

She shivered. "W-what?"

I trailed my hand up her bare arm, up to her throat, brushing my thumb over her pulse point.

"I realised I trust you."

She inhaled sharply.

"I saw you with Granville, earlier." I hissed out the words, unable to hide my distaste for him. "I can't stand that slimy prick, but seeing you with him, the only thing I felt was fucking jealous that he got to speak to you, and I didn't."

I nipped at her earlobe, and she trembled again. "I trust you," I repeated, hoping she could hear that I really fucking meant it.

"Took you long enough," she murmured, the corners of her mouth turning up, and I could feel a smile tugging at my own lips. Bringing my other hand up, I cupped the back of her neck, my fingers tangling in her soft hair.

"I've got another question for you." I drew my head back, just enough that I could see her eyes. "Do you still want to be just friends?"

"I don't want to be your friend," she whispered, holding my gaze. "I never wanted that."

"One last question, and I already know the answer to this."

"Someone's confident." She raised a brow at me, biting her lip to hide her smile.

"We're no longer friends. You're mine, okay?"

"Fuck, yes. That wasn't really a question, by the way."

"You're *mine*, Snowflake," I growled, reiterating my words, and then I couldn't hold back any longer. I slammed my lips down on hers, and she opened her mouth for me, pulling me even closer, her tongue sliding against mine. It was like her kiss set off a chain reaction straight to my dick, and I ground myself into her. Fuck, I'd missed this. I'd missed *her*.

"Cade," she whimpered. "Please tell me we can leave."

"We're leaving, right now." *Before I get fucking carried away and do something stupid like claiming you by fucking you right here so everyone can see you're mine.*

Not that it could be that simple. For a start, I'd been driven to the ball, along with Zayde, Portia, and Jessa, so we'd have to get a cab back to the house, which would be full of people for the after-party.

We made our way back through the ballroom and out of the town hall as quickly as we could, avoiding everyone, but neither of us touching, aware there'd be eyes on us.

"West!" I called to my brother, who, with perfect timing, was holding the door open to a cab, while Lena climbed inside.

He turned around at my shout, a pleased grin forming on his face as he took us both in. "Wanna share our cab?"

Back at the house, the sounds of the party spilled out of the open door. West and Lena disappeared inside, and I turned to Winter. "Feel like getting out of here? I doubt we'll have any privacy, even in the bedrooms."

"Ye—"

I didn't give her a chance to finish before my mouth was on hers again, hard and demanding. I couldn't stop myself. I'd denied myself for too long; I needed her.

Our kiss was interrupted by a low drawl coming from my right.

"Finally got your shit sorted out, then."

Pulling away from Winter, I looked at my best mate, who was smirking at me. "Yeah."

"Good." Zayde threw the stub of his joint on the ground. "Coming in?"

"I might change out of this dress," Winter murmured. "It's not the most comfortable thing to wear. And these heels are killing me."

She slipped past me and headed off up the stairs, smiling at Zayde as she passed.

"Are you two official now, then?" Zayde looked at me curiously.

"Yeah. She's mine, and I want everyone to know it. They so much as think about flirting with her—"

"Chill." He shook his head at me. "No one will try to fuck with her. They know the consequences." Moving back through the doorway into the house, he added, "She's good for you."

"I know. Too good for me."

"That's not true." He frowned at me.

"Whatever. I'm going to change out of this suit. Thanks for, y'know."

He nodded, before turning to walk down the hallway, throwing one last comment over his shoulder as he sauntered away from me. "It's not true. And you're welcome."

For the first time since Winter had been taken, I relaxed. The low rumble of my R8's engine, and my girl, back where she belonged, next to me, as I gripped the steering wheel, navigating the empty roads with ease—this was all I needed.

My eyes slid to Winter. She was watching me, a small smile on her lips.

"What?"

"Just looking at you." She shrugged, acting like it was no big deal.

"You were eye fucking me, Snowflake."

She huffed out a laugh, before her voice turned serious. "Cade. I need to talk to you about the ball."

Not tonight. Tonight, we were going to forget all the shit we were dealing with. Tonight was about one thing only—me and her. That, and how many times I could make her moan my name.

I took one of my hands off the steering wheel and put it on her thigh. Her bare thigh. Stroking my thumb across her smooth skin, I returned my attention to the road. "Let's think about that tomorrow, yeah? I approve of the outfit choice, by the way." I inched my hand up her thigh, under her skirt, and she gave a soft gasp, wriggling in her seat.

"Stay still, otherwise I'll stop," I warned her.

She immediately stopped moving. "Cade..."

"Just relax." My fingers brushed her inner thighs, and it was my turn to gasp. "Fucking hell. You're soaked. *Baby*."

That. Was. It.

Up ahead was a dirt road leading to a tiny car park—

normally used by walkers as it marked the beginning of a trail to a viewpoint about half a mile away. There'd be no one there now, and I wasn't waiting any longer. Pressing down on the accelerator, I felt the car respond, and we were there less than two minutes later. I spun the wheel, turning onto the dirt road, and brought the car to a screeching halt in the empty car park, sending clouds of dust up behind us.

One small problem.

As much as I loved my R8, the interior wasn't exactly conducive to the things I wanted to do to my girl. Too fucking cramped, and she deserved more. Outside the car would do for now, until I could get her in my bed and fuck her until she couldn't walk.

Not wasting any time, I shot out of the car, round to Winter's door, and threw it open. "Come here." My voice was hoarse, my dick begging to be inside her tight, wet pussy.

She slid out of the car, all coy and innocent, fluttering her lashes. She chose *now* to tease me? Fucking seriously?

I gripped her hips, using her body to slam the door shut, and crowded her up against the door.

"Do you know how long I've waited to be inside you again?" I growled the words into her ear, biting at her earlobe, my dick, hard as steel, pressed against her stomach.

"Hopefully the same amount of time I've waited," she murmured breathlessly. "I've come to appreciate my vibrator."

"No. No. No. That's no substitute." I ground myself into her, my hands sliding up, under her top, cupping her tits. "No bra?" My voice was so thick and hoarse I doubted she could even understand me.

"It kind of seemed redundant." Her words ended on a moan as I dragged my thumbs across her hard nipples, then pinched them lightly. "Cade... I missed you so fucking much," she whimpered, gripping my ass and pulling me more tightly against her, swivelling her hips against me, her skirt up around her waist.

This girl.

I was surrounded by her. All soft skin, tight, wet heat, breathy moans and sighs.

All. Mine.

"Snowflake. Fuck, baby."

I slid my hand down between us, teasing her by keeping it over her underwear. She moaned again, her cries loud in the still night air, as I stroked across her slit, feeling her wetness under my fingers. I swallowed her moans as I kissed her, my cock fucking throbbing, painfully hard and straining against the sweatpants I'd thrown on back at the house, needing to be inside her.

Taking my hand from her nipple, I hooked it under her thigh, wrapping her leg around me and aligning myself so my dick was against her pussy.

Fuuuuck.

I bit into her neck, and she turned her head, biting mine in return, running her hands under my sweatpants and digging her nails into my ass. I groaned and pushed her underwear aside, sliding my finger into her pussy as my thumb stroked her clit.

"More," she begged, her voice urgent.

"You want more, huh?" I scraped my teeth up the side of her throat, adding another finger, dragging them both in and out of her tight wetness as my thumb continued to stroke over her clit, her soft whimpers testing my restraint. I needed this to feel good for her, but I couldn't hold on for much longer.

"Cade. I'm gonna c—" I felt her tightening around my fingers, her hands pulling me even closer, as she fell apart for me, her head thrown back, riding my hand like it was my dick.

"More." Her voice was a breathy whisper as she came down from her high, my fingers still inside her. As I slid my fingers out, her mouth met mine, and she kissed me like she fucking needed me to breathe.

She manoeuvred her hand into my boxers, gripping my cock. "Remember what you said to me once, King Caiden?" Her breath came in short pants, her lips almost touching mine, swollen from our kisses.

Not waiting for a reply, she pulled down my sweatpants and boxers in one go, sinking to her knees, licking across my IV tattoo.

She stared up at me from beneath her lashes, her eyes heavy with lust.

"You said, if you were the king, I should get on my knees and worship you," she husked out, then wrapped her lips around my cock.

I swear I saw fucking stars.

Flicking her tongue across the head, she caressed my balls, moving her head backwards and forwards, torturing me with her slow pace, gradually taking my dick inch by inch into her mouth until I was all the way to the back of her throat.

I needed more.

I gripped the back of her head, tangling my fingers in her hair, and thrust into her mouth. She let out a choked moan, the vibrations of the noise travelling straight down my cock.

I thrust again, hitting the back of her throat, and she swallowed, her hands moving around to my ass, holding me in place rather than drawing back. Her tongue dragged along the underside of my cock, and she moaned again, digging her nails into me as she let me set the pace.

Fuck me.

I fucked her mouth, the sight of her on her knees, choking on my dick, tears in her eyes, sending me over the edge. "I'm gonna come," I hissed out, and she just gripped me harder, taking me even deeper, and I came, my dick throbbing in her mouth, cum spilling down her throat, marking her as mine. She stared up at me through her tears, her throat working to swallow everything I had, until I was spent.

On her knees in the dirt, her hair blowing in the night breeze, she'd never looked more like a fucking queen.

She licked around my dick one last time, softly, then released it, rising to her feet, panting. I took her face in my hands, kissing her pouty lips, then kissed the tears that had spilled down her cheeks away, one by one, until they were all gone. Breathless, she collapsed against the side of the car, her pupils huge, turning her blue eyes almost black as she stared at me.

"You're fucking amazing," I told her, meaning every word, and her mouth curved into a smile. "But I'm not finished with you, yet."

16

winter

Caiden picked me up and carried me around to the front of the car, sitting me on the edge of the hood, my legs still wrapped around his waist. My jaw ached from sucking his cock. Not that I was complaining. Seeing him let go and fall apart for me was worth everything, not to mention it had made me horny beyond belief.

"Is this where we fuck?" I spoke the words against his lips, my arms wrapped around his strong back.

I felt him smile against my mouth. "Gimme a minute to recover, yeah?"

"Oka—" I started to say, but my words died away as he slid his hands into my hair, angling my head to the side and running his tongue up my neck. He left soft bites across my jaw, licking away the sting, then bit my earlobe. Goosebumps stood out all over my body, his combination of soft kisses and licks and stinging bites driving me insane with need.

I whimpered. I didn't think I'd ever been so turned on in my life. Knowing how he set me on fire, and being deprived of him for so long, living under the same roof, had been a kind of torture I didn't ever want to repeat. Now, I was desperate for him.

"I fucking missed you." Something in his tone had me drawing my head back, turning to meet his heated gaze. It wasn't just lust burning in his eyes. There was more, a smouldering intensity behind the fire, that made me catch my breath and my stomach flip. My heart rate kicked up, butterflies going mad inside me, adding to the sensations I was already feeling, sending me into overdrive. I kissed him, hard, attacking his mouth, scraping my nails down his back, using my legs to drag us even closer until there wasn't even a millimetre of space between us.

He groaned into my mouth, then ended the kiss, pressing his mouth to my ear. "You ready for me to ruin you for anyone else?"

"Yes," I moaned.

He didn't need to know that he already had.

That one word was all the invitation he needed. He pressed on my shoulders, pushing me back until I was sprawled over the hood of the car, my skirt up around my waist, my pussy soaked for him. I raised my head, watching him as he dug into his pocket and pulled out a grey rectangular object, sliding his thumb up to reveal the blade of a knife extending from the top of the handle, glinting in the dim moonlight shining on us.

"A knife? Really?"

He gave me a wicked grin. "Might've got the idea from Z."

"Of course you did."

My amusement died away as our eyes met, his gaze open, hiding nothing, and I laid my head back, trusting him completely.

I felt the cold press of steel against my inner thigh, and I shivered involuntarily, then held myself as still as I could while he cut my underwear away from me.

"There you are," he breathed, his voice low and hoarse, and then he pushed my legs apart and his tongue was on me, licking up through my wetness, flicking against my clit, his breath warm on my inner thighs as his tongue worked magic. I gripped onto his hair, tugging hard, and I felt him chuckle against me, before he carried on with slow, unhurried licks, adding a finger as he sucked my clit into his mouth.

"Fucking hell," I moaned, involuntarily squeezing my thighs together, trapping him between them. He added another finger, scissoring them inside me, while his mouth...fuck me, *his mouth*. I clamped my thighs tighter around his head, crying out his name as I shuddered beneath him, coming so hard that I forgot where I was, lost in him.

"Look how hard you made me, Snowflake." He pulled me into a sitting position, supporting me with his arms while I caught my breath, weak and boneless from the orgasm he'd given me.

I stared down between us at his cock jutting out between us, ready for me. "*Caiden*." My brain refused to work.

"Do you know how much—" He stopped speaking abruptly, burying his face in my neck, sinking his teeth into my collarbone, and I hissed, both from pleasure and pain. All I could do was sit there, supporting myself on my arms as he slid his hands up under my top, cupping my breasts, stroking across my nipples, then pinching them. He lifted my top and sucked one breast, then the other, covering them with soft bites, sucks, and kisses, dragging his teeth across my nipples, until I was so fucking wet and ready for him that I was once again grinding against him, his dick against my wetness, begging over and over for him to be inside me.

"You want me, do you?" He stared at me, heavy-lidded, his expression a mixture of lust, longing, and amusement.

"I've always wanted you. From the first moment I saw you."

I didn't mean to say the words, but they came out anyway, and I was shocked to find that I meant them.

He didn't reply, but kissed me until I was breathless, dragging the full length of his cock against me, over my clit, up and down, torturing me.

"*Cade.*" His name fell from my lips, a plea, and he reached down to grab a foil packet, ripping it open impatiently. He rolled the condom on, then without warning, suddenly thrust inside me.

Fuck.

He filled me so completely.

I clenched around him, and he growled, biting into my neck, gripping my ass.

He thrust into me, holding me in place as I lay back, feeling his cock jump inside me, his tongue licking across the shell of my ear, making me tremble. The metal of the car was cold underneath me, but Caiden's body was hot against mine. I rolled my hips against him as we kissed over and over, his hands caressing my breasts and moving between us to work my clit as he set a slow, lazy pace, until my lips were swollen from his kisses. I was wetter than I'd ever been, and I was desperate for more.

"I need you to fuck me hard, now, Cade. *Please*." My gasped words were carried away on the night breeze that blew through the car park, but nothing could cool this blazing inferno between us.

My words snapped something between us.

He flipped me over and bent me over the hood of the car, my thighs pressed against the grille as he fisted my hair, his other hand gripping my hip. His muscles flexed against me as he drew almost all the way out, then pumped back into me, and I moaned his name as he pulled on my hair, arching my back as he sank all the way inside.

Our breathing was ragged in the night air, as he thrust into me again and again, harder and faster, and I met his thrusts with my own, holding on to the car, our bodies driving into one another as he fucked me into oblivion.

When I came down from my high and could finally see straight, Caiden brushed my hair to one side, kissing my neck. “You’re unbelievable.” His hoarse words sounded low in my ear, as he pulled out and turned me around to face him. Sitting on the car, my legs shaky, I looked up at his gorgeous face, winding my arms around his neck.

He carefully picked me up and carried me round the side of the car, somehow managing to open my door without dropping me. Placing me down on my seat, he clipped my belt around me, covering my now-shivering body with a blanket that had been rolled up in the footwell.

“Totally worth the wait,” I murmured, once he’d opened his own door and slid into his seat.

“Yeah. I agree.” With a smile playing across his face, he leaned over and kissed my cheek, brushing my hair away from my face, before he started the engine.

I sank back against my seat, my eyes closed.

He completely wrecked me.

Could I say dickmatized?

If this is a dream, don’t wake me up.

The party was still going strong when we pulled into the driveway. Cade motioned for me to stay where I was, then came around to my side of the car and scooped me up, blanket and all. He carried me into the house and up the stairs, ignoring everyone else, not stopping until we were in his bathroom, the door locked firmly behind us. The sound of the running water drowned out the noise of the party—mostly, anyway, and he stripped us both off and soaped my body, still not speaking, his touch sparking the fire back to life inside of me.

I felt his hard cock against my ass and ground myself back into it, and he groaned, sliding his hands around me to caress my breasts as I leaned back against his chest, turning my head to kiss him.

"Do we have time for one more round?" My voice came out all breathy.

"There's always time for one more round." He slid one of his hands up to cup my throat, squeezing lightly, trailing kisses along my jawline.

A loud banging on the door made us both jump, and I screeched loudly.

"Stop fucking and get out here!" Weston's shout came through the locked door.

I pouted and Cade laughed, shaking his head. "Cockblocked by my own brother. Come on. We'll continue this later when everyone's gone."

"I suppose we'd better be social, if we must." I sighed, giving him one last kiss before I left the shower—very reluctantly, may I add.

Time to face the music.

17

winter

In the kitchen, leaning against the island, I sipped my drink while I chatted to a couple of girls from my economics class, idly admiring Cade as he talked to Z and another guy. Every now and then he'd catch my eye, giving me a smile or a cheeky wink, and every time, my heart skipped a beat. We were both wearing jeans, standing out like sore thumbs in the midst of the crowd still dressed in their ball gowns, tuxes, and suits, but to me, he looked better than anyone else in the room. I'd been teasing earlier when I'd called him King Caiden, but the way his presence dominated the room, everyone deferring to him? I wasn't wrong. He was a born leader, someone that other people looked up to and admired. Admired a bit too much, if we were talking about the girls who were constantly vying for his attention.

"You've worked miracles."

I turned around to see Cassius behind me. He motioned with his head, and I said goodbye to the girls, following him out through the sliding doors onto the back decked area with the hot tub, which was mostly empty thanks to the chill in the air. I opened the wooden storage unit we kept outside and pulled out two thick, fluffy blankets, handing one to Cassius, then sank into the reclining chair next to his, huddling under my blanket.

"What do you mean, I've worked miracles?" I picked up the conversation where we'd left off inside.

"Cade. He's, I dunno, happy."

A smile spread across my face. "Elaborate?"

He settled back in his chair, taking a swig from his beer bottle before continuing. "When we were younger, yeah, he used to play up and get into trouble, but he was more like West. More…carefree, I guess? But ever since his mum died, he's been kind of angry and brooding a lot of the time—most of the time, in fact. The whole burden he took on, the responsibility of what happened, and all that shit with your mother… He didn't seem like he had much to smile about, y'know? Until you."

"Me?"

"Yeah. Look at him, in there."

I turned to look back into the kitchen, watching. Caiden spoke animatedly to the guy he was with, then tipped his head back in laughter, playfully punching the guy in the shoulder.

"I like him so much, Cass." My voice came out as a whisper, my emotions overwhelming me.

"The feeling's mutual, babe. He's fucking crazy about you." Resting his beer bottle on the arm of his chair, he sighed heavily, adding, "He's lucky to have you."

"Yep." I smirked at him, and he grinned, his tone lightening.

"Not that I want to be tied down to one woman, but if I did, you'd be top of my list, of course."

"Of course." Laughing, I reached for my drink but stiffened as I glanced over at Caiden again and saw Jessa making a beeline for him, putting her hand on his arm and reaching up to speak into his ear.

I held my breath, watching to see what he would do.

He shrugged her arm off, an angry look on his face, shaking his head and taking a step back from her. She took a step forwards, pressing against him and hooking her arms around his neck.

That. Was. It.

I saw red, shooting out of my chair and storming through the doors, stalking up behind her and gripping a handful of her hair, using it to jerk her backwards. Not too hard, but enough to tell her that I wouldn't take her shit anymore.

"What. The fuck. Do you think. You're doing?"

She dropped her arms from Cade's neck, a look of shock on her face as I spun her to face me. I let go of her hair, glaring at her, and her eyes widened at my expression before she tried to recover, her lips curling into a sneer. "What does it look like I'm doing? I'm spending time with my date. Got a problem with that?"

Unfortunately, with her being in skyscraper heels, and me being in the scuffed pair of trainers I'd thrown on after my shower, the effect I was going for was kind of ruined as I had to look up at her, rather than us being a similar height. Even so, I wasn't about to let her intimidate me. No, I was way, way past being intimidated.

I was raging.

It was a build-up of things. The scathing looks, the catty comments, the blatant hitting on Cade right in front of me... didn't she have any self-respect? And shouldn't women be trying to build each other up, rather than tear each other down?

That final thought was the *only* thing that kept my temper from completely boiling over and slapping the smug, disdainful look off her face.

"Jessa. Listen carefully, because I'm only going to say this once." I stepped closer, my teeth gritted and my fists clenched as I hissed out the words. "You—"

I never got to finish my sentence.

In one quick movement, Caiden brushed past Jessa, moving around behind me, spinning me around and lifting me into his arms, and then his mouth was on mine. My rage melted away, and Jessa was instantly forgotten, as my legs went around his waist and I wrapped my arms around his neck, kissing him back. He flicked his tongue against my lips, and I opened my mouth for him, sliding my tongue against his, my eyes closing. I dimly heard noises around us, as he carried me, holding me effortlessly.

The back of my legs met cool stone, and he deposited me on the marble island, finally breaking the kiss. He pressed his forehead to mine, still holding me tightly, both of us trying to catch our breath.

"I see you." Those same words he'd said to me during the fireworks, spoken with rough insistency, made my stomach flip, and I shivered in his arms as his hot breath fanned across my skin.

He ran his hands up my back, sliding into my hair, his lips brushing against mine, his words stealing the breath from my lungs.

"Only you, Snowflake. No one else compares."

It was around four in the morning when the party ended. People were crashed out everywhere, all over the house—chairs, floors, beds, anywhere there was space. Zayde and Weston had both disappeared, and I'd ended up back outside on the deck with a small group of people—me, Cade, Cass, two guys from uni, both named Mark (yeah, a little confusing, but on the plus side it was easy to remember their names), and four girls—two of whom were currently draped all over Cassius. Cannabis smoke hung thick and heavy in the air, and rain fell steadily around us, beating a soft, hypnotic rhythm on the roof that covered the decking. The area was illuminated by a string of fairy lights which cast a soft glow around the space, and the boys had turned on the patio heaters which were keeping the chill from the air.

I was snuggled into a large recliner with Caiden, one of the fluffy blankets covering our legs. We passed a joint back and forth while we chilled with our friends, the conversation laid-back and flowing. It was so good to be able to be with Caiden again, to be close to him, to not have to keep my distance. None of these people would be bothered about us being together, and I was making the most of it.

Cade took a large hit of the joint, pulling my head towards him. He exhaled against my lips, sending the smoke into my mouth, following it with a soft bite to my lower lip. I smiled up at him, completely relaxed in his arms.

"You must have a magical pussy to tie down Cavendish," one of the Marks commented, staring at me through glassy, heavy-lidded eyes.

"I guess you'll never know." I shrugged, feeling Caiden stiffen behind me, starting to lean forward.

"Leave it." I twisted to face him. "We're all pretty wasted."

He looked down at me, frowning. "No. I—"

It was my turn to shut him up with a kiss. He growled in frustration but eventually kissed me back. I rolled my tongue against his, tasting whiskey and weed, a combination which somehow worked, or at least it did after the amount of weed and alcohol I'd already ingested.

He finally pulled back from me, muttering, "Good thing I like you so much." His jaw was still set, but his gaze softened as his eyes met mine.

"The feeling's mutual." I passed him the remainder of the joint. "Not that you needed me to tell you that."

He exhaled, smoke curling through the air, before he flicked the end off the decking into the wet grass, then turned back to me. "I did. I've been without you too fucking long."

Smiling, I shook my head but said the words he wanted to hear. "I like you, Caiden Cavendish. A lot." I took a deep breath, coming as close as I'd let myself to admitting how strong my feelings for him were. "More than a lot, actually. And I'm beyond glad that you got everything straight in your head. This night ended up way better than I'd imagined."

"Yeah, it did end up being pretty fucking epic." He grinned, his frustration forgotten. "Tell me again what you said about liking me more than a lot?"

"Stop it!" I buried my face in his chest, my cheeks hot. It had been hard enough to say it the first time.

"Say it again."

"No." I kept my face hidden.

Leaning down, he gripped my jaw, angling my head so he could press his mouth to my ear. He breathed out, and flutters of sensation danced across my skin, then licked across the shell, sending shivers through my body.

His voice was a whispered rasp, but I heard it as clearly as if he'd shouted it.

"I like you more than a lot, too."

18

winter

It took the whole morning to clear the remaining partygoers out of the house and then put the house back in order. All on about three hours' sleep. The boys called the cleaning agency, who sent two cleaners over to help, okay, to do 90 percent of the clean-up, reiterating that they needed to be paid double for working on a Sunday. Weston and Cassius had disappeared earlier, giving Lena a lift home, then Weston was collecting a package from one of his mysterious web contacts. It all sounded a bit odd; he was picking it up from the lockers that were held in the local train station—they were the type that you could have packages delivered to from various couriers, and you'd be given a passcode so you could collect your items. Still, I got the need for secrecy, and the fact that these guys could never risk showing their faces, thanks to their activities being highly illegal for the most part.

I'd called Kinslee to see if she was free, and I was finally getting a chance to sit down, now she'd arrived. We were currently curled up on the sofas in the huge lounge, drinking hot chocolate while I ran through the events of the previous night. I'd missed not having her around, and I had so much to catch her up on.

"That's a lot to process." Kinslee stared at me when I finally ran out of steam, tucking a strand of caramel hair behind her ear and picking up her hot chocolate. She blew across the top of the mug, dispersing the steam, then took a tiny sip. "Mmm. So good." Cradling the mug in her hands, she sat in silence for a moment, taking the time to go through everything I'd told her.

"First of all, have you checked your phone today?"

I shook my head. "I've hardly had time to think, what with trying to clear out the house, sorting breakfast for about thirty people, and cleaning up. My poor phone has been very neglected. All our phones have, for that matter. We've been too busy."

"Check it." She looked at me expectantly, and I picked up my phone from the coffee table, where it was lying next to Caiden and Zayde's phones, unlocking it and scrolling through my social media.

Oh.

Among the many photos of the ball and the after-party, it seemed that my kiss with Cade had garnered quite a lot of attention. I'd been tagged in several photos posted by various different people, showing him holding me in his arms, our mouths fused together, completely oblivious to the rest of the world. The pictures actually gave me butterflies—seeing real, photographic evidence of me and him, how wrapped up we were in each other. I screenshot a couple of the best images, happiness filling me as I thought about the night before, how he'd proved to me that he wanted us to be together.

"You're falling for him, aren't you." Kinslee's words were a statement rather than a question.

"Yeah," I said softly, my voice shaky.

She gave me a long, searching look. "I'm happy for you. Just...be careful, okay?"

I nodded, then a horrible thought occurred to me. "Fuck. Kins, what if my mother sees the photos? Or Arlo? Or anyone involved in their deal. I'm not going to be able to talk my way out of this."

"You'd better hope they don't see them. But do you really think they'll care?"

I sighed. "I do. Mostly because of this deal thing Arlo's got going on, and he doesn't want anything to tarnish his reputation. Plus, my mother's already implied how distasteful it would be if anything was to happen with Cade, not that I particularly care about her opinion. I just don't want to mess anything up for Cade. Or for this deal."

"Right then." She put down her hot chocolate and clapped her hands together, making me jump. "Let's see how far the influence of the Four stretches. Hopefully a few calls, and we can make these pictures disappear."

"Great idea." Wasting no time, I jumped up and dashed out of the room, racing into the kitchen. Where were Caiden and Zayde? Basement gym, maybe?

I threw open the door to the stairs that led down to the basement, hearing the distinct sound of gloves on leather. Good.

As I reached the bottom of the stairs, I sucked in a breath, taking a moment to appreciate the sight in front of me, my sexy as fuck man, his gloved hands pounding the set of pads that Zayde was holding up, both of them in shorts with bare torsos. Yeah. I stood there watching them a bit longer than I should have.

"Alright?" Zayde noticed me standing there drooling and raised a brow, and Cade stopped punching, spinning around to face me, his chest heaving from the exertion. Droplets of sweat trailed down the planes of his body, towards his IV tattoo that I could just see the top of above the waistband of his shorts.

So hot.

"What's up?"

I dragged my eyes away from his abs with an effort, meeting his amused gaze, and told them both about the pictures as Zayde put the pads away and Cade removed his gloves. He came to stand in front of me. "Don't worry, we'll sort it." He dropped a swift kiss on my nose, then leaned in closer. "You're such a little tease, giving me those horny eyes. You make it really bloody difficult for me to keep my mind on my workout."

"What you gonna do about it, huh?" I licked my lips, then stood on my tiptoes to press a kiss against his smiling mouth, before staring up at him, waiting for his reply.

"I've got a few ideas. But they'll have to wait for later."

"Break it up, for fuck's sake." Zayde's irritated voice came from behind Caiden.

"Workout time is sacred," Cade whispered loudly, making me laugh.

"Sorry, Z. I'll leave you both to it. Thanks for sorting it, though." I left them to the sounds of Zayde muttering about putting a pin code lock on the basement door and rejoined Kinslee on the sofa.

A while later, the boys came in, picking up their phones and disappearing off to make some calls.

"All sorted?" Kinslee asked, when they finally returned. Cade sank down next to me and tugged me into his lap, sideways on, so my legs were stretched out across the sofa cushions. I curled into him, his body all warm and freshly showered, and he kissed the top of my head before replying to Kinslee.

"Yeah. It wasn't as bad as it looked, really. Most of the photos were of the ball, and everyone's selfies from the after-party."

"What's the fucking fascination with selfies, anyway?"

I turned to face Zayde. "Z. Has anyone ever told you that you're a moody bastard?"

He gave me one of his trademark blank, icy looks, but there was no malice behind it. Still made me shiver, though. Just a bit.

"Leave the poor man alone," Kinslee said. "Come on, Zayde, show me how to play this game."

Cade and I both watched, fascinated, as Zayde actually took the time to explain to her how to use the console controller, and once she got the hang of whatever shooting game they were playing, he seemed to relax, more or less, the tension gone from his jaw, and his mouth no longer set in a hard line. We stayed like that for a while, the two of them becoming competitive in the game, while Cade and I spoke about nothing of consequence, just enjoying this bit of time we had before we had to go back to reality.

We didn't get to relax for long. Around twenty minutes later, Weston and Cassius burst in the door, Weston carrying a cardboard box in his arms, covered in parcel tape. He placed it down on the coffee table.

"This is it. Z, you wanna do the honours?"

At his words, Zayde paused the game, digging in his pocket and pulling out a small object. He pressed it with his thumb and a blade sprang out.

More knives. Why was I not surprised?

He carefully sliced the box open, then sat back, letting Weston take over again. Pure excitement filled his eyes as he reached into the box, bringing out various objects one by one, all packaged in bubble wrap, which he laid out on the coffee table next to the box.

"This is better than Christmas." His grin was contagious, and I couldn't help smiling in return, as he began the tedious task of unwrapping all the layers of bubble wrap.

Cassius sat on the floor, leaning against the sofa, his head next to Kinslee's legs and his own legs stretched out in front of him. "Hey, Kins? You any good at head massages, babe? I've got a banging headache."

She tutted and rolled her eyes, but I saw her smile. "If I must. But you owe me one, okay?"

"Deal."

Kinslee moved, seating herself with her legs either side of his head, then leaned forwards, dragging her fingers through his hair, across his scalp.

He groaned. "Yeah, that's it, baby. Your hands are magic."

"So I've been told," she said dryly.

"You wanna give me a head massage, too?" Cade spoke next to my ear, his voice all low and husky. I was about to reply, when Zayde interjected.

"It's like a fucking massage parlour in here. Next you'll be—"

"Happy endings massage!" Cassius exclaimed, drowning him out. "You up for doing that, Kinslee?"

"No." She swatted lightly at the side of his head before continuing to massage him, and he laughed.

"It was worth a try. Now, West, you ready to show us what you've got?"

I made a mental note to ask Caiden what was up with

Zayde, later. Not that he'd probably tell me, but I couldn't help wondering if something was going on. He'd been more irritable than usual today. Maybe it was me, but something about him seemed off.

Gathering my thoughts, I returned my focus to the items Weston now had out on display on the table, discarded bubble wrap lying around everywhere. I reached for a piece and started popping it absent-mindedly, as Weston shuffled through the objects, inspecting each one carefully.

"Chuck me a bit of that bubble wrap, will ya?" Cass asked in a low tone. I passed him one of the sheets, and he started popping it, too.

Zayde gave both of us an icy glare, and I shrugged, continuing to pop the little air-filled bubbles.

"Focus, Snowflake," Cade muttered in my ear, then kissed the side of my face, running his hand over my stomach to soften his words.

"Sorry. Here, you have a go. It's really relaxing."

He took the bubble wrap from my hands. "I haven't done this for years."

"Can. Everyone. Stop. With. The. Fucking. Bubble. Wrap." Zayde's voice sliced through the room like a knife, sharp and cutting. He sounded like he was at the very limits of his patience, and my head shot up to see the full force of his icy glare directed at the sofa we were sitting on.

Did I ever mention he had serial killer eyes? There they were.

"Fuck, he's scary when he does that." Kinslee shivered, ripping the bubble wrap from Cassius' hands and throwing it over the arm of the sofa where it fell to the floor.

West just stared between us, a kind of wild, trapped look on his face, like he really didn't want to be in here with us.

"Okay, enough. We've had our fun. West. Tell us what

you've got there," Cade commanded, breaking the sudden tension in the room.

"Uh. Everyone ready?" He held up the first item. It looked like a tiny box to me, black and rectangular, reminding me a bit of a car key fob. "GPS tracker."

"What's that for?" Kinslee voiced the question I was about to ask.

"This can go on Christine's car. I have another one for dad's car." He grinned at us, pleased.

"West, that's brilliant! So we'll be able to track where they're going?" I beckoned to Weston to pass me the tracker, and I examined the smooth plastic object with interest, before passing it to Caiden.

"Yeah, if all goes to plan. Just got to put the trackers on their cars without them noticing, which I reckon we should be able to do next time we're at my dad's house."

"Nice one, mate. What's next?" Cass looked at West expectantly.

"Let me see...these."

"Binoculars? That's a bit boring."

Weston rolled his eyes at Cassius' lack of enthusiasm. "Mate. These aren't normal binoculars. They're night-vision ones." He passed the heavy binoculars over to him. "And they're really fucking expensive, so be careful."

"This all feels very James Bond," Kinslee commented, curled back up on the sofa now she'd stopped massaging Cassius' head.

"Is this a good time to bring up code names?" Cassius' eyes gleamed with excitement as he examined the binoculars from every angle.

"No. Please, no," I begged. "I am not getting into another bloody code names argument with you and West."

He huffed but said no more, bringing the binoculars up

to his eyes before recoiling. "Fucking hell, Z. Will you stop with the psycho looks?" Zayde totally ignored him, and he passed the binoculars up to Kinslee, muttering, "Don't look at Z through them."

Weston cleared his throat, shooting Cassius a warning look before returning his attention to the table. "Final item." It was a small, shiny black oblong-shaped object, a bit like a really chunky retro mobile phone. I watched as West fiddled around with it for a moment; then suddenly the sides popped out.

"A drone? Fuck, yes. I need to see this." Cade reached for it, and I kind of zoned out as the Four began discussing camera resolution and flight times, Zayde finally thawing out a bit as they talked. I moved off Caiden's lap, scooting over to Kinslee.

"All this stuff? I really hope it helps us get some answers. I'm so tired of not knowing. I feel like I can't properly lay my dad's memory to rest until I know what happened, if that makes sense."

"Perfect sense." She squeezed my hand gently. "I'm here for you. Whatever I can do to help, I'll do it. And I'm crossing everything that my brother will have some useful information about the *Argo Navis* when he comes home."

"Thanks. And same, I mean, I'm here for you for whatever."

"I know." We both sat quietly for a moment, letting the boys' conversation flow around us, and then she shifted in her seat, angling herself to face me more. "Did you ever google Andromeda, by the way? It kind of stuck in my mind, so I looked into it a bit."

"I did, but I never found anything useful." I sighed.

"You know Andromeda is something to do with space, right?" Her expression was thoughtful. "I might be way off, but I couldn't help wondering about the whole thing with the Argo Navis being a constellation. I know that was a coincidence, since the boat was actually called the *Argo Navis*, but what if Andromeda is a code name or something that your dad came up with?"

"You think?" I eyed her doubtfully, but as I actually thought it through, the more I felt like she could be onto something. "You know what? This could definitely be worth investigating. Maybe there's something I've missed." A thought hit me. "What if his star charts contain answers? Or clues, at least? I never thought to look at them."

She grinned at me. "Dream team, baby."

"You know it. Let's tell the others once we have the charts to hand; I'll come and pick them up in the week." Although I'd moved in with the Four, since it was only supposed to be a temporary arrangement, I'd left some of my stuff back in my room in Kinslee's apartment, including the star charts.

I suddenly realised that the others had stopped talking and were watching us curiously.

"Anything you wanna share?" Cassius stood, stretching, then flopped onto the sofa between me and Kinslee.

"No," I started to say, then stopped. "Actually, yeah. We need to talk about the ball."

I gave them a rundown of my conversation with James. As soon as I mentioned his name, Cade grabbed me and pulled me into his lap, tightening his arms around me possessively.

"You really don't like James, do you?" I murmured softly, while the others were distracted, talking about someone who had got drunk and started a fight at the ball—which I'd completely missed.

"I never liked him, but I have even more reason since

you came along. He used you. He's had his dick in you. I fucking hate him."

I stared into his darkened eyes, hard and angry, but I could see the vulnerability underneath. "We've talked about this before, but you have to know that no one could even dream of measuring up to you, in my eyes. You're not even in the same galaxy." Hooking my arms around his neck, I stroked my fingers through his soft, dark hair as he stared at me silently. "You have to know how I feel about you. James is insignificant to me, to us. A blip in my past. You? You're my future."

His eyes closed, and he groaned. "Fuck, baby. I—" He cut himself off, kissing me with one of his hard, demanding kisses, gripping my jaw to hold me in place. I kissed him back with everything I had.

"I'm getting a boner just watching you two kiss." We sprang apart to see Cassius eyeing us with rapt interest, his face far too close for my liking.

"Cass. There's a thing called personal space." I unhooked my arms from around Caiden's neck and shoved at his shoulder. He laughed and moved away, leaning back on the sofa.

"Let's finish discussing this ball, then you can go do whatever you need to do. And I can go do whoever I need to do."

"Right." I rolled my eyes at him and turned to face the others. "Um. The only other thing I wanted to mention was what happened when I followed Arlo."

I gave them a brief rundown of the events, trying to recall the snatches of conversation I'd overheard.

"I'm not convinced about dad's involvement in all this, but at least now we have this new gear, we might be able to watch the docks more, try and work out what's going on down there." Weston started carefully packaging everything away.

Cade spoke up. "Tuesdays seem to be our best bet. We'll aim for a Tuesday—we'll split up, two of us can go back to Alstone Members Club while the others check the docks, but we need to proceed with caution. Z, you said Creed told you security had been stepped up there?"

Zayde nodded, before swiping the game controller from the floor. Everyone seemed to take that as a sign the conversation was over.

"Kins, you want to help me? You're a girl. I need to buy a gift for my sister. Right now. I've got about half an hour before I need to leave." Cassius turned to her, giving her his best begging look, putting his hands together in a prayer symbol.

"More favours?" she grumbled. "Go on, then. But you owe me. I'm guessing we're shopping online?"

Horror crossed his face as he stood, pulling her to her feet. "Fuck, yes. I'm not going shopping in town or anything. Can't imagine anything worse."

Their voices faded away as they disappeared from the room. Weston finished packaging up the items and followed them out of the door, box in hand.

"Are you okay?" I asked Caiden. He was shifting restlessly, flexing his knuckles.

He nodded, then shook his head. "No. Yeah. Just a bit edgy after all this shit that's happened. You wanna get out of here for a while? We can do a drive-by of the docks, see if we can see anything."

"Sure." I stood. "We could drive through town and pick up food for tonight on the way back. Maybe Thai?"

"Yes."

Climbing to his feet, he held out his hand, and I took it.

19

caiden

The oars dipped through the water with a soft splash as my muscles strained, moving us closer to the docks.

"I can't believe we're in a rowboat." Winter's quiet laugh cut through the night air, as she sat across from me on the bench seat. From his seat in the prow Zayde sat, silent and still, scanning the coastline with the night-vision binoculars my brother had given to us.

Yeah, I couldn't believe we were in a fucking rowboat, either. Z's mates had come through for us, so here we were, cutting through the water, hoping to get close to the docks without being spotted. Security was still tight around the docks' entrance, so this way we could avoid detection. If we were lucky. So far, luck was on our side—the sky was clear, the moon providing a bright enough glow that we hadn't needed to use lights and the sea was calm—it would've been suicide to come out here in a rowing boat in bad weather.

Weston had wanted to come with us, but there was no way I was letting him put himself in danger. I'd asked him and Cassius to go back to AMC instead, to see if they could get any more answers, while me and Zayde took the docks. I wanted Winter to stay out of the way, too, but my girl flat-out fucking refused, stubborn woman that she was. Consequently, my stress levels were at an all-time high; not only did I not know what kind of shit we'd find ourselves in, but I had to worry about her.

Other than that, we were as prepared as we could be—all armed and dressed in black. Yesterday and this morning, Z had taught Winter a couple of basic tricks with knives that she'd hopefully never have to use, because if anyone hurt her, I would fucking end them.

We drew closer to the docks, hugging the coastline, and Z tapped me on the shoulder, handing me the binoculars. Placing the oars down, I scanned the direction he was pointing, until I saw it. The *Argo Navis*, a nondescript, small cargo ship moored in its own berth, away from the other boats. I passed the binoculars to Winter and unpacked the drone, before rowing us closer.

Stopping a safe distance away, I turned on the drone. It hovered noiselessly in the air just above the boat, responding to the controls like a fucking dream. I'd spent yesterday getting to grips with it until I could handle it to West's satisfaction, and now today I was putting my new skills to the test.

Winter leaned around me, passing the binoculars back to Zayde. Before we'd left, we'd agreed that Z would be the lookout, I'd commandeer the drone, and Winter would watch the tiny video monitor that connected to the drone's camera, to see if anything jogged a memory.

Winter crawled across to my seat, the boat rocking despite her slow, careful movements, and I sat her between my legs. I slid my thumb forwards on the controller, and the drone shot off across the sea, while she held the video monitor. Angling my head, I leaned my chin on her shoulder, my face next to hers so I could see the screen as well.

She wriggled against me, and my dick decided this completely inappropriate moment was a great time to wake up, hardening against her ass.

"Sorry," I breathed into her ear. "Can't help my reaction to you."

"I'm not complaining," she murmured, her amused voice laced with heat. "We'll do something about it when we get —" Her voice cut off as she suddenly leaned closer to the screen, and I followed her gaze, holding the controls of the drone steady. She pointed at the top right corner of the screen, where one of the little cranes that was used to lift the cargo off the boats was hoisting something into the air from the deck of the *Argo Navis*. "Do you see that? Can you fly it closer?"

"Yeah." I flew it closer to the boat until it was hovering near to the hull, still keeping it at a safe distance. Even though it was tiny, and noiseless, and a solid black colour which blended in with the darkened sea and sky, it was possible that it could still be spotted.

"Z, are you seeing this?" I hissed.

"Yep." The object became clearer the closer we got. A large pallet, stacked high but completely wrapped in some kind of plastic—it was difficult to make out from here. The deck had more, identical pallets, arranged in neat rows. A figure stood on the docks, gesturing as each pallet was placed down, unhooking them from the crane.

We sat in silence until all the pallets were unloaded, and then the boat shuddered to life, and I flew the drone to the side, hovering over the roof of the building Winter had been held in. Fuck, thinking of her in there, the fact she'd been under our feet all that time, I could kick myself for missing it. Whoever her rescuer was, I owed them. Massively. If only they'd show their face. Why had they kept themselves hidden?

Shaking off my thoughts, I used the oars to move us even closer to the coastline, where there was a thin strip of stony beach, and we waited as the *Argo Navis* moved out of the dock and disappeared out to sea. The drone's low-battery alert flashed up, so I navigated it back to the rowboat.

"Now what? You reckon we should check out the pallets?" I asked Z in a low voice.

He studied the docks through the binoculars for a moment without answering me, before he lowered them. "Yeah, it looks to be safe. I'll signal Creed." Pulling his phone from his pocket, he texted "going in," which would let Creed know we were entering the docks. We'd planned it all to leave as little room for fuck ups as possible—Creed had a couple of his guys waiting in a van a way down the road from the docks, and if Z didn't make contact an hour after the first message, they'd come after us.

That was something we didn't want to happen, but it was our safety net in case it all went wrong.

Rowing the boat around the side of the building, I steadied it, holding it in place while Z jumped out, tying the boat to a chunky iron ring that was cemented into the ground. If we were lucky, no one would spot it.

"What are the chances of you waiting here in the boat?" I tightened my arms around Snowflake possessively, the need to protect her so strong that it overrode everything else.

"Zero, so don't even suggest it." She twisted her head to frown at me, her blue eyes huge and serious. "I'll be careful, I promise. You have to trust me."

"I do trust you, but I fucking hate this whole situation. I can't stand the thought of anything happening to you." I buried my face in her shoulder, and she sighed.

"I know. Same, though. I know you think you're this big, bad, invincible person, but that doesn't mean you can't get hurt." She kissed my jaw, running her hands over mine. "Don't take any unnecessary risks."

"Are you coming, or what?" Zayde's low hiss came from above us.

"Yeah, sorry, mate." I helped Winter out of the boat. We pulled on the balaclavas and gloves we'd brought with us—Winter's idea—and skulked around the side of the building, keeping low to the ground. We used the pallets for cover, keeping behind them with the sea at our backs, in case anyone showed up.

I held up a hand, signalling Winter and Zayde to halt, so we could examine the pallets. I took my knife from its sheath, carefully making a small slice in the wrapping, then digging it in further to reach the contents. Zayde pointed his phone flashlight at the pallet so we could see better.

White powder.

"Coke?" Z pulled a glove off, running his finger over the flat of my knife blade, which was dusted with the powder. Lifting his balaclava, he touched it to his tongue and grimaced. "Yep. It's coke."

What the fuck were pallets full of cocaine doing at Alstone Holdings' docks?

"Are they all the same?" Winter's soft, muffled voice sounded close to my ear.

"I think so, yeah." I scanned the rows of pallets. I couldn't be sure without examining them all, but they looked the same to me.

"You wanna check out the building, again?" Z suggested,

and I glanced at Winter. I could only see her eyes, but they held so much trepidation that I was about to say no, not wanting her to have to relive her experience there, but then a steely glint of determination entered her gaze.

"Let's do it." Her voice was firm, with only the slightest tremor, and in that moment I was so fucking proud of her. My girl was prepared to face something that probably scared the shit out of her, and there was no hesitation on her part.

After a short, whispered discussion, we decided that Zayde would stay by the door as our lookout, and Winter and I would go inside. He took up his position, and we entered the building, turning on our phone flashlights. As we headed down the dusty, dark corridor, Winter swallowed nervously, her hands shaking slightly. I took her hand in mine, and she held on to me tightly as we drew closer to the metal door.

The door was ajar, thank fuck. I grunted as I threw my weight against it, pushing it open enough for us to enter the room. It was empty, just like before. But now we knew there was a hatch in the floor, I scanned the ground with the torch and noticed a dull metallic gleam off to the side of the room.

"There."

I lifted the hatch with a scraping sound that echoed around us, reverberating off the stone walls, and shone my light into the gloom. Rough stone steps led downwards, and I descended into the room Winter had been held in. She followed close behind me, keeping her hand on me the whole time as if to reassure herself I was still there. When we reached the bottom, I looked around until I found the light switch on the wall and turned it on, bringing a dim glow to the room.

"Snowflake?" I turned around, noticing Winter standing frozen at the bottom of the stairs, her eyes filling with tears.

Fuck.

In three strides I was over to her, pulling her into my arms. "Shh, it's okay." I stroked my hands up and down her back, feeling her body tremble against me.

"I'm sorry," she said in a small voice. "I didn't think it would affect me so much. I just...the memories suddenly hit me. Hearing your voice and not being able to do anything, then trying to escape and getting so close, then..." She buried her face in my chest.

"Listen to me." Lifting her chin, I pulled up her balaclava, and mine, so we could see each other properly. "I'm not gonna let anything happen to you, okay?" Lowering my head, I kissed her softly. "I'd take a fucking bullet for you, baby."

Her eyes widened in horror. "Don't tempt fate by saying things like that." Then she reached up and kissed me again. "I'd do the same for you."

Something inside me cracked open at her emphatic words, but I pushed the feeling aside. I had to.

She lifted her hands, tugging my balaclava back down before doing the same to her own. "Thanks for, well, everything. Come on. Let's see if we can find anything useful here."

We explored the room, and I learned just how much fucking restraint I had, digging deep into my reserves as she relived the experience of being held captive down here. Yeah, she'd told us all before, but it was one thing to hear it, and another to be standing in the place it had gone down. I needed to break something, really fucking badly, by the time we'd finished and she'd told me the whole story again.

"You're incredible, you know that?" My voice came out

all hoarse, and I cleared my throat, trying to get myself under control. She needed me to be strong; I couldn't afford to show any chinks in my armour. Not until this shit was over. And maybe not even then.

She squeezed my hand tightly, seeming to sense my mood, tugging me over to a door with a heavy padlock.

"Do you have that lock-picking thingy?"

I nodded and dug around in my zip pocket, pulling out the lock-picking tool. Within a few minutes the lock was open, and we were peering into a storeroom.

"This is a bit weird." Winter scanned the shelves that lined the room. Blankets, clothing, rolls of toilet paper, camping mats, as well as some more sinister-looking items —thick, heavy ropes, chains, handcuffs, and rolls of duct tape. "If we were anywhere else, I'd say all this stuff—" She waved her hand at the ropes, chains and handcuffs. "—was for some kinky shit. But here, it just seems kind of scary." We photographed the room, replaced the padlock, took some photos of the main room, then exited as quickly as possible.

As we were lowering the hatch into place, Zayde burst into the room. "We've got company."

We raced out of the building and skidded around the corner, hearing the rumble of an engine drawing closer, then coming to a spluttering stop. An insistent beeping sounded, and I ducked down, looking around the corner.

A small lorry with no number plates had parked next to the pallets, and a forklift truck, where the beeping was coming from, was lifting one of the pallets up. I watched, using my phone to take photos as a figure opened the back of the lorry, then gestured to the forklift truck driver, and one by one, they transferred the pallets into the back of the lorry.

"My leg's gone dead," Winter groaned quietly behind me, sinking to the floor and stretching her legs out in front of her, rubbing her thigh to try to get some circulation back into it. Zayde chuckled under his breath, alternating between staring around the corner and texting on his phone.

"They're almost done," I commented. The final pallet was eventually loaded, and the back of the lorry was closed. The figure at the back of the lorry spoke to the driver of the forklift truck, and I strained my ears to hear. I couldn't make out anything they were saying, but what I *did* know was that they weren't speaking English.

Once the lorry and the forklift truck had both disappeared, I turned to the others. "Let's get back to the boat and back to the house. Get all these photos and drone footage on the computer."

"Cass and West are on their way back." Z waved his phone in the air.

Winter looked between us both, her gaze all hopeful and determined. "Good. Maybe between the five of us, we can finally get some answers."

After all the shit we'd been through, we'd better.

20

caiden

We studied the charts that were spread across the table in front of us. Weston sat at the computer, searching for information, a large mug of coffee in hand.

"It says here that Andromeda's a galaxy, closest one to our galaxy, in fact, and it's also a constellation." His eyes scanned the screen, cataloguing all the details, before he sighed in defeat. "I really don't see anything here that would help us."

"That was my conclusion, when I googled it." Winter shifted in my lap, her voice sad. I brushed her hair aside and kissed the back of her neck, and she turned her head and gave me a small smile, before staring back at the charts.

"Yeah. I've heard the name before, only in relation to this cybercrime shit that was going on a few years back, but that's nothing to do with this." He slumped back in his chair, rubbing a hand across his face, then straightened up. "No. Fuck this. I'm not giving up. I'm gonna speak to Mercury."

"Snowflake, I'm gonna give West a hand, okay?" She nodded, and I lifted her off me, letting her slide back into my seat, then crossed over to join West at the computers. He was soon connected to the secure chat he used in the deep web, waiting for Mercury to show up. A green light blinked on next to Mercury's name, finally, and West started typing, with a relieved breath.

NITRO: Need some intel.
MERCURY: Details?
NITRO: 2 items. 1: A name/word—Andromeda. Constellation and galaxy have been ruled out unless you see anything suspicious.
2: Sending you footage taken earlier relating to the 2 subjects I asked you to investigate. Might be useful.
MERCURY: On it. Anything I should know?
NITRO: Think all this is linked somehow. But can't work it out.
MERCURY: Give me a couple of hours. Might have some intel on the ring too.

The screen went blank, both of them logging out at the same time. West stretched, turning to me. "Mercury's on it," he said, as if I hadn't been sitting right next to him for the past five minutes. "I want to try hacking into Dad's system again, see if I can find anything. Alstone Holdings isn't showing anything out of the ordinary, and AMC was a complete waste of time tonight."

"This is so fucking frustrating," I muttered. "Did you manage to pull up the employment records for the docks staff?"

"Yeah, but there's no one listed that fits the dead guy. Another dead end."

"All we're doing is getting one dead end after another." I drummed my fingers on the table, needing to do something. Anything. “Is there anything else we can check?”

Not only did I want Winter to find out what had happened to her dad, for definite, I wanted to pin something on Christine, something concrete. It was clear all this shit tied together, somehow. Winter needed answers for her dad, and the rest of us needed to know what the fuck was going on. Were our families involved? What the fuck was happening at AMC, and at the docks?

“Cade. We’re on it.” My brother looked at me with so much conviction, so much trust. He shouldn’t. The familiar feeling of guilt rolled through me, thick and suffocating. I’d become a pro at pushing it down, but ever since Winter had come into my life, it had forced it to the surface.

Fuck.

Glad my brother couldn’t read my thoughts, I changed the subject, before the memories could drag me under. “Anyone want another coffee? Think it’s gonna be a late one.”

“I’ll help,” Cass offered, standing up and stretching with a yawn. I nodded my thanks, and he followed me out of the room.

winter

When Cade and Cass had left the room, and Weston was absorbed in sorting through the cargo records from the docks, I got up and switched to Cassius’ seat, next to Zayde.

“Um...Z?” I ventured. He’d been more irritable than

usual the last few days, ever since the ball, actually, other than earlier tonight, when he'd been engrossed in our mission to the docks. It wasn't really my place to ask him, but I got the feeling that he didn't really have female friends, and maybe I could be that to him. I *was* that to him, at least I thought so, but I wanted him to know that I was there for him.

"What is it?" He spoke without looking at me, scrolling through the photos from the docks on an iPad with one hand, the other flicking his knife blade open and closed, over and over again.

"Is everything okay? I mean. Argh." I huffed out a frustrated breath, staring down at the table. "Tell me if I'm out of line. I just want you to know that if you ever want to talk to anyone, I'm available, or whatever."

His head shot round to look at me, and surprise crossed his features for a moment before they reverted to his usual blank mask. "It's all good. Nothing sleep and a few decent hits from a joint won't cure."

I stared at him, unconvinced, and he held my gaze, giving nothing away, before he flashed me a brief smile. "You're good for Cade, y'know."

"I'm glad you think so." I returned his smile with a big grin, beyond happy that I had the approval of Caiden's best mate. "It means a lot to know I've got your approval."

"Don't fuck it up," he warned, softening his words with another quick smile, before he returned his attention to the iPad.

"I think I've got something."

Weston's tone, full of cautious hope, had us both spinning to face him.

"Tell us," Zayde commanded.

He met Zayde's eyes, then mine. "I've searched through

all the cargo records for Alstone Holdings, going back for a whole year, and there's nothing for Tuesday nights. The other days, apart from Sunday, when everything shuts down, we have records—if not weekly, at least monthly."

Caiden and Cassius re-entered the room with mugs of coffee. "What did we miss?" Cass stared at Weston curiously, while Caiden beckoned to me and I got up, rounding the table to slide into his lap. He banded his arms around me, dragging his nose up my cheek to my ear, where he nipped at my earlobe, before he focused his attention on his brother.

Weston repeated the information he'd just told me and Zayde, then continued. "That in itself seems a bit dodgy, but get this. The user ID for the records on Mondays and Tuesdays is Christine."

"What does that mean? She's the one filling in the records?" I tried to get my head around what he was saying.

"Yeah, or someone logged in as her, anyway." He returned his attention to the screen, scrolling through the cargo inventory and records of supplies in and out of the docks.

What was going on?

"West. How long until Mercury gets in contact?" Caiden's voice sounded close to my ear, all low and husky, distracting me from my thoughts.

"Maybe ninety minutes or so?" He shrugged. "Not sure."

"I'm taking a break," Caiden announced. Then just for my ears, "Come with me."

In his bedroom, he shut and locked the door behind us and then crossed to sit on the edge of his bed, tugging me onto him so I was straddling his thighs.

"I've been wanting to do this all fucking night, ever since

the boat," he said roughly, gripping my chin and angling my head, then slanting his lips across mine.

I melted into him, kissing him back, and he ran his hands up and down my body, before gripping my hips. His cock hardened between my legs, and I ground into him, relishing the friction, a frustrated moan escaping my lips as he thrust up into me, our clothes an unwelcome barrier between us.

"You're so fucking brave. And sweet. And sexy. And mine," he rasped between kisses, his hands moving from my hips to my top, lifting it over my head before he continued kissing me.

Breaking the kiss, I slid my hands under his T-shirt. Pulling it off, I ran my hands all over his torso, feeling his muscles bunch and flex under my fingers, all hard planes and smooth skin.

"How did I manage to snare the king?" I nipped at his neck playfully, and he laughed against my shoulder as he pinched my nipple between his thumb and forefinger, sending a jolt of heat straight to my core.

"Guess you got lucky." He stood, holding on to me, then tipped me onto the bed, pulling my leggings and underwear off. "Or maybe I'm the lucky one."

I stared up at him, drinking in his gorgeous body as his eyes raked over me, darkening. He licked his lips. "Yeah. Definitely me."

"Cade," I begged.

He gave me his slow, sexy smirk, the one that did funny things to me, then dropped his trousers and boxers. Palming his cock, he kneeled in front of me, pushing my legs apart. "Fuck. Look at you."

Crawling between my legs, he dragged his cock against my soaked pussy, then tapped the head against my clit before slowly rubbing and teasing me, driving both of us insane with lust.

"What are you doing?" I moaned, breathless, reaching down between us. He gripped my wrist before I could touch him, throwing his body weight across mine. Locking both my wrists together above my head, he stared at me, our faces so close that his lashes were touching mine.

"I love playing with you," he admitted in a low voice, his lips curving into a smile. "I don't...I never cared before you."

I pretty much melted. How and when did he turn from an angry, brooding alphahole to this? My heart. He was killing me with his words and his actions.

"Carry on, then," I managed, hooking my legs around his ass. He tilted his head to sink his teeth into my neck, his grip on my wrists tight and secure as he left bites all down my neck, grinding his cock against my wetness until I was on the edge of an orgasm, and he wasn't even inside me yet.

I tried to free my wrists, growling when he didn't let me go, and I felt him laugh against my shoulder.

"I'm gonna come, and I need you inside me." I ground myself into him, tightening my legs around his ass, so fucking wet and ready for him.

He finally freed my wrists, and I raked my nails down his back, making him shudder against me. "Condom," he said hoarsely, the crack in his voice telling me how close he was to losing control.

"I'm on the pill, and I'm clean. I want to feel you come inside me."

"Fuuuuck." He drew the word out on a long, low moan. "I'm clean. Fuck. You're sure you want that?"

"Yes, so fucking sure." I slid my hand between us as he lifted his hips, positioning his cock, then thrust inside. I was so wet he slid in easily, and my eyes rolled back as he buried himself inside me, the sensation indescribable.

Sex with Caiden? Mind-blowing.

Sex with Caiden without a condom, feeling every single part of him, skin to skin?

Out of this world.

"Faster. Harder." I urged him on as he thrust in and out of me with long, powerful strokes, the feel of him inside me completely overwhelming. I was already so close to the edge, that when he reached between us and pressed against my clit, my orgasm tore through me, powerful and all-consuming. As my pussy tightened around his cock, it sent him over the edge, and his hot cum filled me, a sensation I'd never experienced before, taking my breath away.

I wanted more.

More of *him*.

He devastated me.

"Oh, *fuck*." Trying to catch my breath, shaking, I pulled him closer to me, kissing his neck as he buried his face in the pillow, our bodies sticking together.

"Yeah. That sums it up." He pulled out of me slowly, raising himself up on his elbows, then rolled us onto our sides facing each other.

Reaching his hand up, he brushed my hair away from my face. "We'll shower and clean up in a minute. Stay here with me." Tugging me more tightly to him, he ran his hands up and down my back.

I curled into him, the aftermath of the orgasm leaving me sleepy and satiated. "Remember when you said you'd ruin me for anyone else? If you didn't before, you definitely have now."

I could practically feel his satisfied smirk against my forehead. "I always follow through on my promises."

21

winter

Back downstairs, Zayde had disappeared, and Cassius and Weston were in the middle of a heated discussion about code names. Again. Bored, waiting, I started scrolling through my social media on my phone, while Caiden went to make another coffee.

Just when I was about to take a closer look at a photo that had caught my eye, my phone rang, Kinslee's name flashing up on the screen.

"Hi, Kins. What's up? How come you're still awake?"

"Late night. My brother got home, and when I saw you were online, I wanted to tell you what I learned from him while it was still fresh in my mind."

I leaned forwards in my chair, grabbing the notepad and pen I'd been making notes on earlier. "Okay. Tell me."

"There's not a huge amount to tell. He didn't get to work on the *Argo Navis*; apparently whenever it turned up, it used to be as he was finishing his shift, and it was always in another part of the docks. But what he *did* tell me was that the dead guy—at least, it sounds like our man, going off the description you and him both gave me—his name was

Vasily. According to my brother, he kept to himself most of the time. He was the security guy in charge on Tuesdays—he'd mostly either be in the guard hut at the entrance, or patrolling the docks."

"Did he say anything else?" I scribbled down what she'd told me already, glancing up at Caiden and giving him a smile as he slid a mug of coffee in front of me.

"He mentioned Petr."

"Petr?" Caiden raised a brow at me, and I mouthed *Kinslee* to him. He nodded and moved over to sink into the chair next to Weston.

"Again, he didn't say much, just that Petr worked at the docks—mostly driving the cargo on to the warehouses or wherever. He said Petr was friendly with Vasily, though. That was pretty much it."

"Okay." I tapped my pen on the notepad. "Thanks for finding that out for me. I appreciate it."

I could hear the smile in her voice. "What are friends for? Sorry I couldn't be of any more help." She sighed into the phone. "Anyway, listen, remember I told you we were going to be away for Christmas—we're leaving tomorrow morning, early. Far too early. We'll catch up properly when I get back, okay? Just try and stay out of trouble."

"Ha. I'll try." It's not like I went looking for trouble. Some of the time, at least. "Have fun with your family. See you for New Year's."

We said our goodbyes, and I recounted the information she'd given me to the boys. Weston immediately logged on to his secure chat, leaving a message for Mercury with the details, and then started going back through the Alstone Holdings employment records with Caiden and Cassius.

As soon as I unlocked my phone, a photo appeared. The image that had caught my eye when Kinslee had called me.

I studied it, fascinated.

It was simply captioned "Gone, but never forgotten." Smiling at the camera was a younger-looking James, maybe around sixteen or seventeen, with his arm slung around the shoulder of a grinning red-haired guy. Next to him, laughing and clutching the arm of the red-haired guy, was a beautiful, ethereal-looking girl with shining blonde hair, and next to her was Joseph, a smile I'd never seen before on his face as he held one arm around the girl, and the other raised in a toast, a glass in hand. James had been tagged in the photo, which was how I'd seen the image, since even after everything, I'd remained friends with him on my social media accounts. Mostly to keep an eye on him, if I was honest.

Swiping through the tags on the phone, I tried to find out who the other people were in the image, but James and Joseph were the only ones tagged, and the photo had been posted from Joseph's account, by the looks of it. I then scrolled through the comments, but it was full of hearts and kisses and messages of condolence, no details.

"Um. Who are these people?" I held up my phone in the air, turning my screen to face the boys.

Caiden turned around, and his eyes darkened as he took in the photo, storm clouds rolling in, his jaw set. He crossed over to me and tugged my phone roughly from my grip.

"Hey! Be careful." I frowned at him, but he ignored me, his entire focus on the photo. Cassius came to stand beside him, his face turning to a stony mask as he viewed the image.

What. The. Fuck.

"Can someone please tell me what's going on?" I stared between them.

Finally, Cade passed the phone back to me, leaning over my shoulder to point at the screen.

"James Granville. Joseph Hyde." He indicated the two I already knew.

"Thanks for pointing out the obvious. Who are the other two, though?"

"They're, uh." He cleared his throat. "Hyde's brother and sister."

"Joseph has a brother and a sister?" Now I could see the sibling resemblance. They looked younger than him to me.

"Had." The word was dragged from Cassius' lips, low and sombre, and a kind of sick feeling filled me.

"What do you mean, had?"

Cassius and Caiden exchanged glances, a whole unspoken conversation going on between them, before Caiden closed his eyes, scrubbing a hand across his face. He blew out a heavy breath and turned to me, as Cassius crossed back to Weston and began speaking to him in a low tone.

"Come with me." He took my hand and led me out of the room and out through the kitchen onto the back deck, guiding me into one of the large outdoor chairs. Tucking a blanket around us, he lit a joint, inhaling deeply, before he passed it to me.

"What I'm about to tell you goes no further, okay?"

I nodded, worried by his serious expression. He stared out at the darkened garden, unseeing, lost in memories.

"Right. You know how we have all the cameras and shit everywhere? That's not only for normal security reasons. It all started the summer we first moved into this house. We have this whole rivalry with the Hydes and Granvilles; it's been going on for years and years. More so the Hydes, to be honest, at least more recently, although the families are both related."

James had referred to this rivalry at the ball, so this part wasn't new information, but I kept quiet, letting him speak.

"At school, we were always playing pranks on each other, getting each other into trouble—mostly me and Z taking the fall."

He sighed heavily again, his mouth setting in a flat line. "Okay. Mostly me. When we'd left school and moved into this house, Hyde stepped up his games. Him and his brother wanted us gone. Sounds dramatic, I know, but our families were at war. We fucking *hated* each other."

"What happened?" I passed the joint back to him and pulled the sleeves of my hoodie down to cover my hands. Even under the blanket, snuggled into Caiden's warm body, I was fucking freezing.

"There was an...incident. Look, I don't know the details, but Tim—that's Joseph's brother—he died."

My eyes flew to Caiden's. He continued to stare straight ahead, but his arm tightened around me. "He's *dead*? How? When?"

"I—I don't know. We don't speak about it. The girl in the picture? That's Hyde's sister. She went off the rails when he died, had a complete breakdown. Her parents shipped her off to some rehab place, and she's never been back since."

I didn't know what to say. I guess that explained Joseph's hatred of the Four, though, if they'd had a long-time rivalry, and he'd lost his brother. Caiden continued speaking. "After that happened, we came to a mutual agreement that there'd be a ceasefire, whatever you wanna call it. There's been nothing since. Until—" He gritted his teeth. "—the shit with you and Granville happened."

"So why now?"

"No fucking clue."

"And you didn't retaliate because of the Alstone Holdings deal?" I guessed. He glanced down at me quickly, biting his lip, before his gaze flicked away.

"Yeah..." He trailed off, shuffling a bit in his seat.

"Cade?" I twisted around to face him, bringing my hand up to his cheek to get him to turn to look at me, running my thumb across the light stubble on his jaw. "Are you keeping something from me?"

He shivered, muttering, "Your hand's freezing." With yet another sigh, he finally met my eyes, his expression shuttered. "I confronted Granville. I couldn't let it lie. He fucked with you and me, and he needed to know that was unacceptable."

Oh. "When was this? What did you do? And why didn't you tell me?" I tried to keep my voice even, but I was getting kind of fed up about being kept in the dark.

"Snowflake...I can't stand that look you're giving me." He scrubbed his hand across his face. "It was at the ball, and I only hit him once, as much as I wanted to pound his fucking face in. I didn't tell you because I didn't want to cause any more trouble between us, not when I'd only just got you back. Then things have been going really fucking well between us, and..." He shrugged helplessly, his mouth twisting, and I swung my body over his to straddle him.

"Cade." I kissed him, threading my arms around his neck, and he pulled me to him, burying his face in my shoulder. "Look at me a minute." I waited until he lifted his head and his eyes met mine. "I know you, and honestly? I think you've been really restrained with the whole James thing. I've been expecting you to retaliate, and I'm actually impressed and shocked that you only hit him once. Of course, now I know about the thing with Joseph and his brother dying, I understand why you didn't do more. What I'm kind of sad about is that you kept secrets from me."

"Fuck. I'm sorry. No more secrets." He wrapped his arms more tightly around me, kissing my head softly. "Not from me, anyway."

Yeah. Maybe not from him, but I had the feeling there were a lot more secrets to reveal, before we got to the bottom of whatever was going on with my mother.

"Mercury's online." Weston's words cut through the silence in the room.

Finally. I put down the playing cards in my hand, making my way over to the computer.

"For fuck's sake, I had a really good hand," Cass muttered from behind me. Mercury had sent Weston a message earlier to say that with the new information on Vasily's name, he needed a bit longer to gather intel, so we'd been playing poker to pass the time.

"Even so, you know Z would have won." I cut a look at Zayde, still sitting at the table, a large pile of poker chips in front of him. As I caught his eye, the corners of his mouth tipped up in a tiny, satisfied grin.

Sitting on Cade, I focused all my attention on the computer screen as the words appeared in the chat box.

MERCURY: No intel on Andromeda, total dead end. We have info on the rest - sent you Vasily Ivanov's dossier. Someone went to great lengths to hide info on him & Petr. Short summary: cousins, both part of the Belarusian Strelichevo crime syndicate. Streli sigil is on the sovereign ring you sent me photos of.

Connections with larger criminal gangs in Russia & Poland.
NITRO: Thanks. Any connections with Alstone Holdings other than Petr's employment?
MERCURY: This is where it gets interesting. No record of Vasily connection so that's a dead end. BUT I hacked Petr's accounts. Large quantity of money paid in and out, both transactions this month. Traced the account numbers. Offshore accounts. Couldn't get much info but I have names of the account holders.

We waited, staring at the screen, watching the blinking cursor. My heart was racing. Eventually Weston started typing, none of us able to wait any longer.

NITRO: ???
MERCURY: Sorry. Out: Nikolay Stravinsky. Right-hand man for Mikhail Strelichevo aka big boss man. In: Christine Clifford.

22

caiden

After that piece of evidence, we knew we needed to speed the fuck up with our investigations. Today's job—distract my dad and Christine while West planted the trackers on their cars. Winter knocked at the door, and it was opened by Allan, my father's long-time butler.

"Allan." I nodded as I passed, and he returned my nod, inclining his head at me, and gave Winter a small bow. She smiled brightly, happy to be moving one step closer to justice for her dad. We hoped.

As arranged earlier, Weston called over to us as we were heading into the house. "I'm gonna check the leak on your car, Winter. Catch you inside in a few." Winter gave him a wave, and we walked inside, Allan closing the door behind us.

"How've you been?" I made small talk with Allan as we moved through the house, heading to the small sitting room where my father and Christine were apparently waiting. Winter walked a couple of paces behind us. It was shit, but we had to act like nothing was going on between us. No point adding to the drama.

"Well, thank you. Other than a cough I can't seem to shake." He coughed hoarsely as if on cue. "Excuse me."

Winter made an effort to join in with our conversation to seem polite when Allan stopped and waited for her to catch up with us. "Thank you. Uh...sorry about your cough. Honey and lemon helps, I find." She stared awkwardly at him and continued. "Sooo...how long have you worked here, Allan?"

"Nine years, Miss Huntington," he answered politely, and I could see her cast around for something else to say, her politeness coming across a little unnatural, and clearly making them both uncomfortable. Sighing under my breath, I distracted them by asking Allan his thoughts on Chelsea football team's latest transfer, and she shot me a private, grateful smile.

Allan showed us into the small sitting room, then disappeared. My dad looked up from his position on the brown chesterfield sofa as we entered, tablet balanced on his knee and his reading glasses on.

"Caiden. Winter. No Weston?" The table lamp next to him threw shadows across his face, making him appear older, almost weary.

"He'll be in in a minute. Just checking something on Winter's car." I lightly caressed the back of Winter's hand with my finger, where my father couldn't see, then crossed over and took a seat opposite him.

"Where's Chr—my mother?" Winter asked hesitantly. The plan was to keep an eye on them both. Of course, my dad had security and cameras and all sorts of shit, so we could never be too careful, but we'd planned everything to eliminate as many risks as possible. Winter's car had been parked next to her mother's car, behind my dad's, and since there was no reason for anyone to be suspicious, we were hoping West could get away with planting the trackers undetected. They were easy to place—under the wheel arch, attached by a powerful magnet, they took only seconds to put on.

"Your mother's in the dining room. Choosing new curtains, apparently." My dad shrugged. "Why, when there's nothing wrong with the ones we have. I'm at a loss."

"Should I go?" Winter directed her question at my dad, but it was me she was really asking. My dad and I both nodded, and she slipped out of the room. I watched her go, admiring her sexy ass swaying in her tight jeans as she disappeared, then turned back to my dad to find him studying me with a frown.

"While I can't say I miss the days of blatant hostility between the two of you, I'm not sure I like the way you were looking at Winter just then, Caiden. Please try to remember, she's your stepsister and not one of your bimbos. Anything you say or do reflects on myself and your stepmother." He levelled me with a severe look. "Need I remind you, I'm in the process of negotiating a huge contract for Alstone Holdings, and we can't afford even a whiff of scandal."

I rolled my eyes. "I know. You remind me every fucking time I speak to you."

"Language." His sharp tone reprimanded me.

"Sorry." I made an effort to calm down, leaning back in the seat, trying to appear relaxed. "How are the negotiations coming on, anyway?"

The frown left his face, replaced with an almost pleased look, and he placed his tablet down, giving me his full attention. "They're going well. After the Christmas break, I'm confident we should be able to wrap things up fairly quickly, all being well. By the end of January, at the very latest, I'd say. The De Witts are responding favourably to our negotiations, and as long as all goes to plan, this deal will mean we'll not only be able to expand internationally, but we'll be able to source high quality construction materials directly from the De Witts estates in the Netherlands, which will mean a huge decrease in the costs that eat into our profit margins."

"Great. Let me know if there's anything I can help with," I said, mostly to be polite. Then added, "But no more setting me up on dates with Jessa De Witt, whatever you do."

He smirked at me, the bastard. "Not a fan? I seem to remember you being all over each other last summer."

"That was before."

"Before what?"

Before Winter came along and showed me what it was to care about a girl as more than just another hole to fuck. "Before I realised how fu—how irritating she is."

He chuckled, shaking his head and picking up his tablet. "Keep that opinion to yourself, but I can't say I'm surprised. The De Witts aren't my favourite people, but we've got to keep them sweet for now. I'll do my best to keep you apart, but if you could at least stay civil—that would be appreciated. I'm sure her father has told her the same. This deal will benefit us all greatly."

I wondered what he'd think if he knew my girl had come after Jessa, pulling her hair and practically spitting fire. Best keep that little piece of information quiet. I smiled to myself. I fucking loved Snowflake's jealous moments. It reminded me she cared—not that I encouraged the attention, but hey, I couldn't help who I was. And she knew I wasn't interested in any other women. How could I be, when she owned every part of me?

"Yeah, I'll stay civil. Don't worry, Dad, I won't purposely fuck things up for you."

"Language," he reminded me, and then he looked at me. *Really* looked at me, like he was seeing me for the first time. "You've...grown up lately, son. Ever since Winter came into our lives, you and Weston are getting on better, and I'm actually seeing you more frequently than a five-minute visit every couple of months. I'm proud of you."

I stared at him, momentarily shocked into silence, then said the first sentence that flew into my head. "It wasn't that infrequent," I muttered. "But thanks."

We looked at each other a bit awkwardly for a minute. This wasn't us; we didn't talk like this. In fact, I couldn't remember him ever telling me he was proud of me before. Maybe when I was a kid, but not that I could remember. That was always down to my mum. She was the one who encouraged me and showed me love.

Fuck. Would the pain of losing her ever go away?

Before I could let my thoughts go down a really dark fucking path, I stood, crossing to the silver tray that held the whiskey. "Drink?"

Of course, with the arrival of Christine, things inevitably went downhill. Snowflake came strolling in with her, chatting easily about fabrics or some shit, playing her part well, and maybe it was the fact we couldn't show that we were together, but all I wanted to do was get her home and bury my dick inside her. She was so fucking gorgeous, but so unaware of it, or of the effect she had on me. Except for the times I was grinding my hard-on into her. I laughed to myself, and she raised a brow at me, amused, which in turn made me laugh more. What the fuck was I doing, sitting here laughing to myself like some lunatic? It wasn't even funny.

I rolled my eyes at myself internally and focused back on the present. "Did you manage to sort the problem with Winter's car?" I turned to my brother, who had finally reappeared and was lounging on the sofa next to me, legs kicked up on the coffee table.

He nodded, all casual. "Yeah. There were two small problems, but I sorted them both. Easy job."

Good.

"Nice one, bro." I held up my whiskey, and he clinked his Coke against my glass—he was driving us home, so no drinking for him. Me, even the slightest contact with Christine drove me to drink.

"Not just a pretty face, am I?" He grinned, clearly proud of himself. As he fucking should be. My brother, the genius.

"Yeah, you're alright for some things." I elbowed him and he elbowed me back, laughing, like we used to do as kids. When was the last time I'd felt this relaxed in my childhood home? Even Christine couldn't ruin it.

Spoke too soon.

"Caiden, I thought I asked you to dress more appropriately for your visits here." She looked over me, her haughty, disdainful gaze making me want to punch something. Clenching and unclenching my fists, I caught Winter's eye. Her gaze, imploring me not to make a scene, was the only thing that kept my temper in check.

I spoke through gritted teeth. "That was for meals. This is a casual get-together."

Surprisingly, my dad spoke up, and all of us stared at him, probably with identical expressions of shock on our faces. "Christine, leave it, please. Let's try and have one evening as a family without jumping down each other's throats."

Her mouth snapped shut, and she pursed her lips, folding her arms, clearly fuming, but not saying another word.

Fucking finally.

My brother elbowed me again, and I glanced at him to see him mouth *what the fuck?* at me. I shrugged, just as baffled as he was.

"Anyone fancy a game of cards?" Winter's tone was hopeful, and just like that, my anger left me. I stared between her and her mother. How could I have thought they were alike? Christine was so fucking prickly, she was practically a cactus. Winter was all soft lips, soft hair, soft skin, and a fucking spine made of steel. My girl could walk through fire and come out the other side without being burned.

"Stop looking at Winter with that loved-up expression on your face. Dad's gonna notice," Weston hissed to me, interrupting my thoughts.

Loved-up? What the fuck kind of face was I making?

"I'm having an early night," Christine announced. Just like that, my evening got better again. She got up and left, still in a sulk, giving us a general goodbye accompanied with an exaggerated huff that left all of us rolling our eyes. Other than my dad, that is. He had his nose buried in his tablet again.

"Arlo?" Winter tried again, waiting until he looked up.

"Yes, dear?" He eyed her over the rim of his glasses.

"I asked if anyone wanted to play a game of cards. Nothing too taxing—we could play Crazy Eights, or something?"

He glanced at his watch and then back at his tablet

screen. Then back at his watch again. He was going to say no, I just knew it.

"I can squeeze in one game. Cards are in the bureau over there."

I was *not* expecting that.

Later, in bed, lying on my back and idly playing with Snowflake's hair while she languidly traced her fingers over my tatts, done in after the three orgasms I'd given her, I voiced the question that had been on my mind all evening. "What was with all the being friendly with Christine and inviting my dad to play cards?"

She wriggled a bit so she could look up at me. "More, now than ever, I don't want Christine to have any reason to suspect us of being suspicious of her." She yawned, her voice sleepy, and I kissed the top of her head. "The cards thing—I thought it would be good for you all. Try and, I don't know, build bridges or whatever."

"It's a bit late for all that, but thanks for trying." I kissed the top of her head again.

"Yeah, but you had a good time, didn't you? If your dad isn't involved in this shit with my mother, you're going to have to work with him after uni. You have to find a way to relate to him. As equals. In business, at least. I just thought, maybe if you started chilling out around each other more, it might help."

"You're fucking amazing, you know that?" I pulled her on top of me, putting my arms around her.

"I have my moments." She smiled, biting my lip playfully, suddenly less sleepy.

Time to take advantage of it. I rolled us over so she was pinned beneath me, my cock hardening against her.

"Again?" Her voice had turned husky, and her blue eyes had darkened, and fuck if it didn't turn me on even more.

"One more time."

She raked her nails down my back, marking me, and I hissed, scraping my teeth down her neck, which never failed to turn her on. Her words came out on a moan. "Cade. One more time with you is never enough."

I stared into her eyes as I buried my cock deep inside her, watching her lashes sweep down, her mouth falling open as she moaned my name again, and I swear my heart fucking jumped. Why did I get this feeling in the pit of my stomach every time she was near me?

Fuck. The realisation hit me like a ton of bricks.

I was falling for this girl. Hard.

23

winter

Me and Weston were sitting in front of his laptop, watching a little blinking purple dot move across a map, as we tracked my mother's car. Arlo's green dot was stationary—he was in the office, and the car hadn't moved all day.

Cassius was following my mother's car, at a discreet distance. He was actually driving Kinslee's car—she'd left the keys for us to use it while she was away, because we figured that out of anyone's cars, hers would be the least recognisable since it was a nondescript, silver VW Polo hatchback, nothing to make it stand out from any other car on the road.

As Cassius trailed my mother, he was texting us via the speech recognition on his phone, keeping us updated.

Cass: Do you see this?
Me: Highnam? Do you think she's headed to the Crown & Anchor again?
Cass: Bet she is. Duck I lost her.
Cass: Bloody autocorrect.

Cass: OK got the map up. I can see where she's going.

There was silence as we watched the moving dot; then it suddenly stopped and started moving back in the direction it had come from.

Me: What's going on?
Cass: She burned around.
Cass: Turned.

My phone rang, Cassius' name flashing up on the screen.

"Thought it was easier to phone. Autocorrect's a fucking joke on this voice recognition thing." His voice came through the speaker, loud and clear over the muted hum of traffic around him.

"What's going on, mate?" Weston leaned closer to the phone, keeping his eyes on the laptop screen.

"Dunno. She was driving, then pulled into a layby and turned around. Good thing I was stuck a few cars back so I could see her turning and follow her. We're—hey, the docks are down here. Fuck, I'm gonna have to drive past; I'll go as slow as I can, but there's a car right up my ass, flashing his lights at me. Bellend!" he shouted, making me jump. "What's the fucking rush?"

"Chill, Cass." West huffed out a laugh. "Keep your eyes on Christine."

"Dickhead," he muttered. "Not you, the driver behind me," he added, after a pause. "Okay, she's turning into the docks, she's stopped...and I'm...okay, I'm past it now. There was a man leaning into her window—I only saw the back of his head, nothing special. He had a bit of a bald patch, I think, or it could've been the light. I don't know really; I hardly saw him. I'll turn around up here and drive back past, see if I can see anything else."

We waited, hearing the sound of the indicator as he turned off the road and headed back in the opposite direction. His voice came through the speaker again, excitement in his tone. "I just saw her standing there with Littlefinger! I mean, Petr. She was showing him something on her phone, I think. Looked like it, anyway. Visual proof she's still meeting up with him."

"I wonder what they're doing," I mused aloud. "Can you turn back round?"

"Already on it. I don't wanna risk going past too many times, though, otherwise someone might notice."

Silence.

Then, "Fuck, fuck, fuck! I think Petr was watching me as I went past that time. His head turned and everything."

"Shit, come back now."

"I fucking am. Gonna ditch the car in the uni car park and pick mine up, then I'll be home." The phone went dead, and Weston and I stared at each other.

"I really hope that was just his paranoia. At least we've seen my mother with Petr, in person. So we know she must still be working with him, because he doesn't work at the docks anymore, does he? There'd be no reason for him to be there unless it's to do with her."

Weston nodded. "Yeah. I'm adding this to our file, with times and dates." He pulled up the login to his secure storage server and started tapping away on the keyboard.

While he was busy doing that, I tried to make myself useful by doing a Google image search on the Strelichevo sigil that had been on Vasily and Petr's rings. I trawled through countless pages of search results, but nothing came up other than one site that Google auto-translated, and appeared to be someone's travel blog. The writer referred to some kind of burial ground, accompanied by a grainy photo of the image on a set of iron gates. I bookmarked the site just in case, but it was only a few lines long.

Through a combination of useless directions, and my own ineptitude, I ended up outside this private burial ground early this morning, while trying to find the cemetery my great-grandmother was buried in. I snapped a photo of the gates, rather unusual and ornate in design, and exited the car to see if I could look around inside. Unfortunately, my attempt was thwarted by a large man carrying a gun, who told me I was trespassing on private property.

The blog then went on to describe, in tedious, rambling detail, the person's journey through various deserted Belarusian roads and how he kept getting lost every few miles. Probably should have invested in a satnav.

Closing my browser with a sigh, I put my phone down and went to make a cup of tea while we waited for Cassius to return.

Why did we always end up with more questions, and no answers?

24

winter

Christmas came and went without incident. Alstone Holdings closed down from Christmas Eve until January 2nd, and Arlo and Christine had flown away to some luxury ski resort, leaving us to spend Christmas alone, which was actually the best thing for us. I couldn't think of anything that would ruin Christmas faster than being forced to spend it with my mother.

Me, Cade, and West spent the day lazing around, watching TV, and we ordered Chinese food rather than cook anything. We'd decided not to give gifts to each other, either —to be honest, none of us felt all that much like celebrating. I was missing my dad even more, and we were all feeling kind of discouraged by the fact we had just as many questions as answers when it came to my mother.

Z was spending the day with his dad, and Cass was with his family, so the house was kind of quiet and subdued. In the evening, West shut himself in his computer room, talking all things computery and gadgety with Mercury and his other dodgy web contacts, so Cade and I reacquainted ourselves with the hot tub. Twice.

Now it was New Year's Eve, and we were going to what was apparently the traditional New Year's Eve party, hosted by Cassius' family. They had a sprawling mansion, very different to Arlo's. It was nestled into the cliffside, all shiny and modern with floor-to-ceiling windows and several different levels, starting at the clifftop and gradually moving down the side. If I could compare it to anything, it reminded me a bit of Tony Stark's *Iron Man* mansion.

According to Caiden, when it had been built, the locals had petitioned against it, saying it spoiled the scenery and general feel of the area, which was predominantly Georgian and Victorian buildings. Unlucky for the locals, since the Drummonds were a founding family of Alstone Holdings and therefore controlled the land, there was nothing they could do about it. I could see both sides of the argument, but there was no denying this mansion was bloody beautiful. All sleek lines and sparkling glass. I bet it would look amazing from the sea.

Speaking of the sea...I'd arrived at the mansion early since the boys were off doing some male-bonding shit, paintballing, and Lena had asked Cassius to ask me if I wanted to come over. Pretty starved for some female company after a week of testosterone with no Kinslee, I'd jumped at the chance.

Time to kick off the New Year's Eve celebrations, Lena-style.

Lena and I were standing at the foot of the cliff on a tiny pebble beach, the mansion high above us. You know what this mansion had? An outdoor lift. I had no idea such things existed until that moment in time.

The beach had a little jetty with a motorboat moored to it. Lena skipped down the jetty, pulled the cover off the boat, and climbed inside.

"Coming?" She cocked her head at me, the ends of her formerly blonde hair, now a shade of pastel pink, tumbling from under her beanie hat and blowing in the breeze.

I nodded slowly, tugging my own hat further down over my ears. "Are you sure you know how to drive one of these? Or is it sail? Whatever it is, we're not going to die, are we?"

A loud laugh burst from her, her thin shoulders shaking under her down-filled winter coat. "You should see your face right now. You look fucking terrified." Fumbling around in the boat, she grabbed an orange life jacket and threw it to me, clipping one on herself, then spun around, stretching her arms out. "See? We're safe."

I stayed rooted to the spot, and she sighed, rolling her eyes. "Winter. I promise we'll be fine. I've grown up by the sea. I've been hanging out on boats since I was a baby. I know everything there is to know about this boat and the coastline."

"Okay. I guess." I took a hesitant step forwards, then another.

"Come on! It'll be fun. The view of the house from the sea is amazing," she said coaxingly. "You don't want to miss it."

Finally, I was in the boat, life jacket on, holding tightly to the rail that ran around the side. Lena unhooked us, or whatever the nautical term was, and started the motor with a roar, a huge excited grin on her face.

I squeaked but tried to play it cool, although my hands were shaking. I'd barely met Lena, hence my coming here earlier, but she came across as the tiniest bit crazy. Flying us across the water at full throttle, she was clearly in her element, standing, legs braced, hands on the wheel, her pink hair whipping around in the breeze.

When I got used to the motion and the speed, I realised I was actually enjoying myself, and I sat back in my seat with a smile on my face.

"You alright?" she shouted to me over the noise of the engine, glancing back at me, and I stuck my thumb up at her. We got a good distance away from the coastline, and she cut the engine.

Then suddenly, everything was calm and still. The first rays of the setting sun danced across the water, and the only sounds around us were the waves lapping at the hull of the boat, and the distant sound of seagulls back by the cliffs.

"Turn around," Lena instructed, and I spun to face the cliffs.

"You were right," I said breathlessly. The house looked like it glowed. The setting sun was reflected all over, from the glass front to the roof. We stayed, just watching the colour change from gold to a burnished orange, and then Lena announced it was time to go back.

"We don't want to be out here in the dark. You want a go at steering on the way back?"

Why not? "Okay. Thanks. I have no idea what I'm doing, though."

"You'll be fine," she assured me, starting the motor back up. "I'll do most of it; all you need to do is worry about steering."

We headed back at a slightly slower pace, and once I got a feel for the responsiveness of the wheel, I steered us back in a gently curving S shape, until we neared the jetty and Lena once again took over. She expertly brought us to a stop, tying the boat up and pulling the cover over it. "That was great, I'm glad you came over. It's fun hanging out with someone older. My brother doesn't normally let his girlfriends anywhere near me."

I laughed. "Thanks for inviting me. But FYI, Cass is not my boyfriend. A close friend, sure. I love him. But not in that way."

We entered the metal cage housing the lift, and she pressed the button that would take us back up the side of the cliff to the house. "I know you're Cade's girlfriend. But you'd have made a cool sister-in-law. Just saying."

Hearing myself be referred to as Caiden's girlfriend put a huge smile on my face. I knew he called me his girl, and we were exclusive, but I didn't think we'd ever referred to each other as boyfriend and girlfriend before.

I liked it. A lot.

Showered, using the bathroom in Lena's bedroom, I finished blow-drying my hair and dressed in the short, tight, sparkly black-and-silver dress I'd bought for the occasion. A knock sounded at the door just as I was smoothing it down, hoping it covered enough of my legs to look like a dress rather than a top. I'd rather not end up flashing my underwear at Cassius' parents if I could help it.

"Come in," I called, and in walked Lena, carrying a metal case in her hand, a bottle tucked under her arm, and a pair of champagne flutes dangling from her fingers. Back in black again, she had on a short pleated skirt, with fishnet tights and chunky platform shoes, and a loose black T-shirt that hung off one shoulder. It had a sparkly sequin skull on the front, so I guess it was kind of festive. For Lena, anyway.

"Thanks for letting me crash here. Are you sure it's okay?" I asked as she carelessly shoved a computer keyboard and a large pot of colourful pens aside, placing the bottle and glasses in front of the huge monitor on her desk.

"Yeah, it's going to be fun. We all squash in together on New Year's Eve—saves getting a cab home. We'll probably end up with a few more girls in here." She expertly popped open the champagne and managed to pour us two glasses, all without spilling a drop. Carrying my glass and the case over to me, she set them on the bedside table. "There's yours. Let's do make-up."

We both beamed at each other. I'd never really done the whole getting ready for parties or nights out with my friends until I'd met Kinslee, and it was fun to be girly and just hang out and play around with make-up for a change.

"You're not going for the whole goth look tonight, are you?" I teased Lena, as she sat herself on the bed next to me.

"It's New Year's Eve. I might introduce a bit of colour to my make-up palette." Opening up the case, she started pulling out various tubes and pots, holding them up to my face. She looked so happy, I just let her get on with it.

"I so wish I had a sister," she sighed, brushing a base layer over my face with a soft sponge.

"Yeah, me too. I was an only child; it was just me and my dad, so I don't even know what it's like to have siblings." I sat silently, eyes closed as she brushed a base over my eyelids, then continued. "Saying that, it was nice, being just me and dad. And now, although I miss my dad so fucking much, and I still cry myself to sleep sometimes, I have this whole family who I'm not related to by blood but I feel closer to than anyone else. Your brother being one of them. You're lucky to have him."

She gave another sigh, then pulled a face. "Yeah, I suppose. I bet he annoys me more than you, though."

"Oh, I'm sure he does. Isn't that what big brothers are meant to do?"

"Yeah. Speaking of my brother." She lowered her voice, even though no one else was in the room. "He mentioned you were in hospital. Are you, you know, okay? I didn't really know you to ask before, but I wanted to know."

I nodded slowly, not sure what to say. "I'm all good. He told you what happened to me?"

"No," she was quick to reassure me. "It was an accident, really. We were doing one of our video chat things where he likes to phone me and annoy me about homework or whatever. West appeared in the background when we were talking, and I heard him say your name, and he asked if Cass could drive him to the hospital. I don't think he realised Cass was on the phone."

"Oh, okay. Yeah, I had an accident. But I'm fine now. Totally healed."

She eyed me for a moment, a torn expression on her face, clearly wanting to ask more, but at the same time, unsure whether she should. After a moment her face cleared, and she squared her shoulders. "Good. I'm glad you're okay." Handing me an eyeshadow palette, she changed the subject. "Pick a colour, and I'll do your eyes for you."

We were interrupted by a knock at the door, and both called "come in" at the same time. A mass of caramel hair, curvy body, and sparkly gold dress barrelled in, and I shouted, flinging myself off the bed and launching myself at Kinslee. We hugged each other, laughing, before I pulled back, flopping back down onto the bed.

"I wasn't expecting you to get here until later." I pointed towards the champagne bottle on the desk as she stepped out of her shoes.

"Just gonna grab a glass," she called over her shoulder, heading into the bathroom and returning with an empty water glass, which she filled with champagne and held up towards us in a toast. "Cheers! Yeah, we left early because heavy snow was forecast, and my brother didn't want to drive back through it." She sank to the floor, stretching her legs out. "Anyway, don't let me interrupt you guys. Carry on."

"Do you two know each other?" I asked curiously, knowing that Kinslee hadn't mixed in these circles before I came along. They both shook their heads—they knew who the other was but had never been officially introduced.

After ten minutes or so, we were all chatting like old friends, thanks to Kinslee's natural warmth and open, friendly demeanour. The champagne was going down nicely, and Kinslee had persuaded Lena to try a different make-up style. Still heavy on the eyeliner, because that was just Lena, but her long lashes were curled and she had on sparkling silver eyeshadow and a sparkly lip gloss on her lips, which were painted a pale pink to match her hair. I had similar makeup, only with less eyeliner and more glitter. I then dusted us all with shimmering powder that I found in the make-up case, and just for fun, sprayed glitter spray in our hair.

"We look like disco balls," I commented as we stood in front of the large mirror in the corner of the room.

"We have to bring the sparkle, it's New Year's Eve. Let's do a selfie to commemorate the occasion. Shoes on," Kinslee commanded and stepped back into her skyscraper heels. I grabbed my stripper shoes, as I called them—the kind with a clear plastic heel and platform sole—and slid them on my feet, making me feel tall for a change. Kinslee stood in the middle, me and Lena either side of her with our arms loosely linked around her, our champagne glasses held up in our other hands, and we took a series of selfies, pouting and laughing and blowing kisses at the camera.

"Who knew being all girly could be so much fun?" Lena mused as we made our way down the corridor and up the white polished stone stairs to the upper floor where the main party was happening.

Kinslee laughed, linking her arm through Lena's. "Not me. But I can safely say, we are totally doing that again."

I was about to reply when a familiar shiver went down my spine, and as I emerged on the upper floor, my gaze was drawn straight to his.

Fuck. Me. Sideways.

25

winter

All the Four were there, but I barely noticed Kinslee and Lena greeting the others. Caiden was the same—his whole focus was locked on me, and he looked at me like he wanted to devour me. I gulped, a nervous excitement thrumming through my veins, my heart beating faster as he sauntered closer. He was all casual, graceful swagger, but I could see the beast in his eyes that he was trying to restrain.

He had on dark, inky-blue jeans and a jet-black shirt that matched his raven hair, the top button undone and the sleeves rolled up to expose his tattooed forearms. There was a bruise, most likely from the paintball, blooming on his cheekbone, and I could see another through the tattoos on his left arm. The bruises somehow made him look even hotter than normal. His eyes were all thundery, full of dangerous promise.

Reaching my side, he spun me around, pressing up against my back, grinding his hard cock into me, his hands on my ribs just below my breasts. "You look so fucking hot, Snowflake. I wanna lift this sexy dress up, push your underwear aside, and fuck you up against those windows in front of us until you're screaming my name." He bit my earlobe, then just breathed across my ear, sending a wave of shivers through my whole body, and I couldn't stand it anymore. I'd seen him for a total of thirty seconds and I was already so wet I'd need to change my underwear. And I needed him. Right. Fucking. Now.

"Umm..." My brain literally refused to work. He nudged me with his hips, pushing us along.

"This way." He walked us down a corridor and stopped outside a door with a key code panel. Punching in a six-digit number, he waited for a second until we heard a click as the door unlocked, and then he reached around me and pushed it open.

We were in a room, dimly lit by some kind of tiny light that had come on automatically when we opened the door. Don't ask me any more than that. All I knew was my boyfriend was spinning me in his arms, hoisting me onto a table, and pulling off my underwear.

"So fucking wet for me already." He stopped for a moment, staring at me lying there, desperate for his touch, and he gave me a feral grin before lowering his head. Then he had his tongue in my soaked pussy, and I moaned in relief, digging my hands into my thighs to stop myself gripping onto his styled hair. When he sucked my clit, I almost levitated off the table, and when he combined flicking my clit with his tongue with his fingers, curling, pumping, and scissoring inside me, I came hard and fast, clenching my thighs around his head, my legs weak and shaking.

"Fucking hell, Cade." My voice came out weak and breathless. "What a way to say hi."

He gave a dark chuckle, grabbing tissues from the box

on the table and using them to clean us both up. The outline of his hard cock looked almost obscene, trapped in his tight trousers, and I sat up, reaching out and running my hand up and down his length. "What's it gonna be, Caiden? Hand? Mouth? Pussy? Ass?"

His eyes flashed, and he bared his teeth at me. "I'm in the mood to mark what's mine. Window. Hands on the glass."

I climbed off the table, my legs still shaking, and stood in front of the window, placing my palms flat on the cool glass. He came up behind me, and I heard his trousers unzipping, and then his cock was pressed against my ass.

"You are the sexiest woman I've ever seen in my life." For a moment he let his emotions show in his voice, as he dropped soft licks and kisses all down my neck and along my collarbone, his hands sliding up under my tight dress to caress my breasts, then back down, one circling my clit while the other came up to lightly grip my throat. Then his grip tightened and his finger moved faster, and he bit and sucked at my skin, marking my neck.

"Fuck, yes." He licked across the broken skin. "I want to leave another right..." He dropped to his knees and spun me around, and I fell back against the window using it for support. "...here." He left his mark on my inner thigh, then licked over it, soothing it, before getting to his feet and spinning me back around and bending me over, then thrusting inside me without warning. I cried out as he fucked me, barely any time before he was coming. As I felt him empty himself inside of me, his fingers worked my clit, playing my body like an instrument he was the master of, bringing me over the edge with an orgasm that left me shaking and breathless. Again.

"Hi," he said, turning me back around and kissing me

for the first time since I'd seen him. Just one, soft, hello kiss, but it gave me butterflies.

"Hi back. At the risk of ruining the moment, I really need to clean up since you came inside me, and that stuff doesn't stay in place."

"You mean my cum? Nice." I heard the laughter in his voice as he grabbed a handful of tissues, passing them to me, before he let out a groan. "These paintball bruises fucking hurt. Worth it, though." He straightened up, stretching. "Come on. Let's get back to your room and clean up. We'll use the back staircase; we can avoid most of the guests that way."

I looked around the room, finally becoming aware of my surroundings. "What is this room, anyway?"

"Cassius' dad's office," he said casually, as if it was no big deal.

"*What*? Are you serious? B-b-but," I spluttered. "That means you ate me *on his fucking desk*! And look at his window!" I groaned, seeing the smeary handprints, glitter, and other marks I really didn't want to think about marring the crystal-clear glass. I didn't dare to look at the desk.

"Don't worry about it. He won't be using it until the day after tomorrow, when work starts up again. The cleaners will have been in here way before then."

"Are you positive?" I tugged my dress back into place, then crouched down and swiped my underwear from the floor.

"I'm sure." He was completely unconcerned, taking my hand and leading me to the door without a care in the world. "Let's go."

"How did you know the pin code, anyway?" I wondered aloud.

Closing the door behind us, he reset the pin pad

before leading me down a mostly empty corridor, through a door, and down a set of narrow stairs to the floor below. "He's had the same code for as long as I can remember. Me and Cass used to sneak into his office as teenagers to watch porn—it was the only computer without parental blocks."

"Ugh. I wish I hadn't asked."

Back in my room, once we'd both sorted ourselves out and were ready to rejoin the party again, he pulled me to him, gently gripping my face in his hands.

"I don't know what came over me, earlier."

"I do. Me. I came over you." I smirked at him, and he rolled his eyes, kissing the tip of my nose.

"Think you're funny, do ya? No, what I meant is, I saw you, and you were all fucking beautiful and I dunno, I couldn't think. I needed to have you. To mark you as mine."

"Well, you did that." Moving my hair out of the way, I indicated the love bite on my neck. He kissed it softly, then drew back to look at me, his expression uncertain.

I hurried to reassure him. "Hey, you didn't see me complaining, did you? I love that people know I'm yours, Cade. I know we have to be discreet in front of a lot of the people here, and I just hope no one saw us together before we went into Cass' dad's office, but just seeing that mark—people will know that I'm taken."

His expression cleared. "Good. I want them to know you belong to me. You're *mine*." Tipping my chin up, he rubbed his thumb over my pulse point, then dropped a hard, possessive kiss on my lips.

I locked my arms around his waist. "I know. I hate that we can't be together in the open. I honestly don't think many people would be bothered; after all, a lot of our uni friends know. I think. But we just have to be patient till this deal goes through, especially here, with some of the key players at the party."

He sighed, pulling me closer to him and kissing my head. "You're right. And we'd better get back, before people get suspicious wondering where we've disappeared to."

With that, we made our way back to the upper floor to rejoin the others.

26

winter

Back in the midst of the party, no one seemed to have noticed our absence, or if they had, they didn't mention it. Caiden left me with Kinslee and Lena, but not before brushing my hair back off my shoulder so my love bite was on show. I rolled my eyes, but like I'd told him back in the bedroom, I loved that he'd marked me as his. I chatted, danced, and drank, having fun, constantly finding my gaze drawn to Caiden's. I couldn't stop smiling like a lunatic, and neither could he.

"Come on, stop eye fucking your boyfriend, and let's get more drinks." Lena tugged on my arm gently, and I followed her from the room, leaving Kinslee dancing with Cassius—apparently she was protecting him from a "psycho clinger" who wouldn't take no for an answer.

We found Estella Drummond, Lena's mother, in the kitchen, and Lena made a beeline for her. "Mum? We need more champagne."

She turned to face us, a gracious smile on her face. Lena and Cassius both took after their dad, looks-wise—Estella was short, curvy, and dark-haired while Lena and

Cassius were both tall and blond. "There's plenty more in the cellar. Help yourselves, but don't drink too much, please, Lena."

"Alright," Lena muttered with an eye roll, and added, "Thanks, Mum," at my nudge.

We turned to leave the kitchen, almost running into someone coming in the door. He looked so much like an older version of Joseph Hyde that I stopped dead, a gasp falling from my lips.

He looked down at me, and a strange, indecipherable expression stole over his face, before it was wiped away and he strode past me without another look.

"Was that Joseph Hyde's dad?" I asked Lena in a low voice, as we headed in what I assumed was the direction of the cellar.

"Yeah. It's a weird one. You'd expect to see the Hydes and Granvilles at general events, since they are part of the Alstone elite, after all. But for some reason, my parents always invite them to their New Year's party, too. They don't like to leave anyone out. And between you and me, my mum thinks their whole rivalry is silly."

"How did the rivalry start, anyway?" I followed Lena into the small lift at the end of the hallway, and she pressed a button marked -3. The lift began to descend with a shudder.

"No one can really remember. It was generations back, now. I think to begin with it was to do with the land ownership, and it all went to shit from there. Now they're business rivals; although Alstone Holdings is so big and powerful now, the Hyde/Granville family can't really hope to compete. And since my family, along with the Lowry and Cavendish family, run the business, and pretty much run this town, they kind of hate us."

The lift doors opened into a cavernous cellar, with

shelves full to the brim of bottles of wine and barrels stacked all along one wall.

"Huh. Money does strange things to people, doesn't it?" I mused. "And by the way, this cellar is insane! Are we actually inside the cliff?" I ran my hand down the rough rock surface of the wall, the stone cold under my palm.

She shrugged. "It does, and yes we are. But without the money, we wouldn't be here right now."

I hummed non-committally. Sure, this house was literally like something out of a movie, and the Drummonds were clearly beyond rich, but was all the hassle worth it? I couldn't answer that. I'd never been in that position to judge either way.

Lena interrupted my thoughts by directing me down an aisle, tall shelves either side of us, and began piling bottles into my arms. "We may as well take a load up with us. They won't last long, with the amount of people drinking."

"Uh... Lena? These are kind of heavy," I warned her, when my arms were aching and I genuinely didn't think I could hold any more without sending them all crashing to the ground.

"Oh, sorry." She placed the bottle she'd been about to dump on me back on the shelf and indicated for me to follow her back out to the lift, her own arms full. I silently prayed that I wouldn't trip in my heels.

Back upstairs, somehow with all the bottles intact, Cassius and Weston came to our rescue, taking the bottles and setting them out. Cassius reserved one of the bottles, a huge grin on his face.

"Watch this," he said to me, heading back into the room where most of our university friends were gathered. He stalked over to the gas fireplace, pulling the samurai sword that hung on the wall down from its holder thing.

"What the fuck is he doing with a samurai sword?" I muttered to West, as he placed the champagne bottle on top of the polished white stone mantelpiece and stuck two fingers in his mouth, sending a piercing whistle into the room to get everyone's attention.

"It's a katana," Weston informed me.

"Whatever it's called, what's he—"

Cassius stood at the front of the room, and with one smooth motion, sliced the top off the bottle with the sword. "Cheers!" he shouted, and cheers echoed through the room as everyone congratulated him on his skills. I smiled to myself, stepping back to the side of the room as he threw me a cheeky wink, a wide, satisfied grin on his face.

"Hi." The voice in my ear sent a shiver through me, and I turned my head to look into Caiden's stormy eyes, his body heat warming me as he slid his arm around my waist. Butterflies raced through me as he pulled me further back into the shadows, against the wall, and dropped his head to lick across my love bite. A soft whimper slipped from my mouth, and I gripped onto his arm, his muscles flexing under my fingers. Fuck. How and when had I fallen so hard for him? Tonight seemed to have solidified my feelings, and all I wanted to do was tell him how I felt, but I held off. If I pushed him, if I tried to make demands of him too soon, he would close up, I knew it. He had to be the one to admit his feelings first.

"Having fun?" I tried to act casually, but I think the tremor in my voice gave me away.

"I am now." He nipped my ear, then licked at the shell, and all I wanted to do was leave the crowds behind and be alone with him, preferably naked. "Are you gonna kiss me at midnight?"

"Yes." There was no way I was going to miss that. I'd never actually had a New Year's kiss before, believe it or not.

"Good. I'll come and find you later." He released me after kissing me just below my ear, flashing me a quick grin. "Stay out of trouble." Then he was gone, swallowed up by the crowd, and a shiver went down my spine.

Not the good kind of shiver. I turned my head, my senses on high alert, and saw Joseph Hyde watching me with a dark, almost malevolent look on his face. I glared straight back at him, daring him to try anything, knowing that the Four would have my back. He dropped his gaze, bringing the half-empty bottle of Patrón he held to his lips and taking a swig, but I could feel the hostility rolling off him.

Choosing to ignore him, I joined Kinslee on the makeshift dance floor. We were then joined by Cassius and Weston and amused ourselves trying to outdo each other with crazy made-up dance moves. By the time I remembered Joseph again, he was gone.

"Damn, that was it." Kinslee shook the empty champagne bottle, tapping the bottom, as if more would magically appear.

"I'll find Lena and see if we can grab some more." I caught a flash of pink hair in the crowds and threaded my way through the masses to Lena. "We're running low on champagne. It's getting close to midnight, so I'm thinking we probably won't need much more."

She nodded and scanned the room. "Okay. This side looks like it still has plenty, so we'll just grab another three or four bottles."

I followed her into the hallway and back down towards the lift.

"Can you wait a minute? I want to use the loo first."

"I'll go on down and get the bottles, if you want," I offered. "I'm pretty sure I can carry them myself, anyway."

"Are you sure?" She looked torn.

"Course. Meet you back up here in a few minutes." I gave her a reassuring grin, which she returned with a grateful smile, and waved her off, before pressing the button to call the lift.

Lost in thought, I wasn't paying attention to my surroundings as I entered the cellar.

If I had, I might have noticed the sound of someone breathing, a shoe scuffing the floor, the presence of another person in the cellar with me.

Strong arms came around my back, pinning me, and a hand clamped over my mouth.

I panicked, thrashing around, trying to throw my attacker off. I was dragged backwards, then suddenly released, and I stumbled, falling into the rough stone wall and scraping all down my arm.

That fucking *hurt*.

Spinning around, reacting on pure instinct, I lashed out at my attacker, raking my painted nails down his face.

"You little bitch," he hissed, holding the side of his face and glaring at me.

"Joseph?" I clapped my hand over my mouth. Then rage overtook the shock as I realised what he'd just done. "What the *fuck* are you playing at?"

He took a threatening step towards me, then another, pinning me against the wall. Alcohol fumes assaulted my face as he brought his mouth to my ear, his speech slurred. "I'm here with a warning. You came here and fucked things up for a lot of people, Winter Huntington."

My heart was beating wildly. No one knew I was here, other than Lena, and she wouldn't be expecting me back straight away. He was too strong for me to fight off.

"What do you mean, fucked things up?" My only option was to keep him talking and hope Lena came to find me when I didn't appear with the champagne.

"Our lives were just getting back to normal when you showed up. Thanks to Cavendish's interest in you"—he spat the word "interest," and I almost gagged as I got a face full of tequila breath—"and you poking your nose where it doesn't belong, we've been forced to intervene."

"What?" My head was spinning. "Who's 'we'? Intervene with what? And by who?"

He ignored my questions. "I'm telling you this for your own good. Stay. The fuck. Away. From Cavendish. Keep your head down, work hard like a good little student, then when you've graduated, get the fuck away from Alstone."

"Oh, and you're threatening me, someone who's weaker than you, because you're too scared to say this to Caiden, are you?" I was a little bit scared, but I was mostly angry. And getting angrier by the second, as he held me pinned in place, his grip tight and bruising, his veneer of civility shattered.

"Shut up," he hissed in my face, clamping his hand over my mouth. Not tightly enough; I managed to sink my teeth into his flesh, and he yanked his hand back with a screech.

"You fucking *bitch*." His hand came out, and with a crack, he slapped me across the face, hard.

Tears streamed down my cheeks, the whole side of my face stinging from the slap.

"*Shit.*" He looked horrified at what he'd just done.

Too late for regrets. How fucking *dare* he?

"Fuck you," I spat, my words turning into a sob, the tears clouding my vision, my cheek on fire, throbbing. "How—"

He suddenly let out the most inhuman scream, and then he was ripped away from me.

27

caiden

Ever heard the saying the red mist descended? I'd been in a fuckload of fights before, but until I saw Joseph Hyde raise his hand to my girl, I'd never experienced it—that all-consuming rage that blinded me to everything else except the need to make him fucking pay.

"I'm gonna fucking *kill you*!" I roared, yanking him backwards, my arm around his neck in a stranglehold, knocking him to the floor and punching him with all my strength. My fists pounded him over and over as he tried to throw me off, hitting me weakly. His drunken blows connected with the bruises I already had from paintballing, but I barely noticed the pain.

Arms pulled me back, lifting me off Hyde, and I gradually became aware of Cassius and Zayde both talking at me, holding me back.

"Caiden!" I blinked, my unfocused gaze sharpening as Cass got all up in my face, blocking my view of Hyde. "Caiden!" he repeated, his voice urgent. "Winter needs you."

My head snapped round as everything came back into focus, and the sound of her soft, choked sobs assaulted my ears, sending a rush of pain searing through me. I took a step forward, needing to punish the one who caused her hurt, the rage building in my veins once again.

"No. Go to her. I'll deal with him." Zayde's voice was like deadly, freezing ice. Cassius dragged me over to Winter, before running to the lift where Lena was about to enter the cellar. He pushed her back into the lift before she could see anything, slamming his hand on the button to take them back up.

I crouched down next to Winter, carefully scooping her into my arms. Her whole body shook with sobs—she was probably in shock, and she curled into me, her eyes tightly closed.

Standing, I carried her to the lift. As the doors closed behind us, I looked back to see Joseph Hyde lying prone on the floor, his face a bloody, beaten mess, and Z standing over him with his knife out and a savage, diabolical grin on his face.

Winter lay curled on the bed in Cassius' old room, where I was supposedly meant to be crashing later along with the rest of my boys. I wiped down her grazed arm with an antiseptic wipe, wincing as her whimpers turned to cries of pain.

"Sorry." I leaned down, brushing her hair away from her face and kissing her head softly. "I know it stings, but I've got to clean it." Rage filled me again as I took in the redness all down the side of her face. What the fuck had Hyde been doing? I hope Z fucked him up so much, he'd never even think of hurting my girl again. Any girl, for that fucking matter.

"Here." Cassius returned to the room, my brother in tow, handing me a bag of ice wrapped in a soft tea towel. I placed it on Winter's cheek, holding it in place, and she hissed, then let out a relieved sigh, her cries growing quieter as I stayed with her, holding the ice with one hand, running my other hand up and down her back and over her hair, soothing her.

"What the fuck happened?" Weston's eyes were full of worry, but as I told him what I'd seen, they darkened, a fury that I'd never seen before descending. "I'm going to end that fucker," he hissed out through gritted teeth, breathing hard. Cass and I both stared at each other, taken aback. Maybe my brother was more like me than I realised. Maybe he was just better at keeping a lid on it.

"Z's taking care of it," Cassius assured him.

"Good." He made a clear effort to calm himself, the anger finally dissipating, and he sat down on the bed, taking Winter's hand and squeezing it lightly.

Dimly, I heard shouts and cheers coming from outside the room.

Cass glanced at his watch. "Midnight in five."

"Go. We'll be alright on our own." I glanced up at Cass and my brother, both looking torn. "Really. Go. You wanna see the fireworks?" And just to lighten the heavy as fuck atmosphere I winked at West and added, "I hear Lena's looking for someone to kiss at midnight," earning a glare from Cass and a smirk from my brother.

They disappeared out of the room after assuring me they'd be back soon, and I stretched out on the bed next to Snowflake. She'd stopped crying, and she moved the ice pack off her face and rolled onto her back, staring at the ceiling, unseeing.

"Why?" Her voice was choked, and just like that, tears

filled her eyes again, and I could quite happily murder the bastard who made her cry. She was so fucking strong, and to see her fall apart like this killed me. I leaned over her and carefully kissed, licked, and wiped away the tracks of her tears, stroking through her hair, no fucking clue how to make it better but needing to try. Fuck. I'd do anything for this girl.

"I won't let him hurt you again," I promised her. We needed to talk about what exactly went down between them in that cellar before I got there, but that could wait.

The distant sounds of the New Year's countdown drifted through the closed door, and Winter swallowed hard, her eyes finally meeting mine. "I don't want to miss my first New Year's kiss," she said in a scratchy voice.

Who was I to deny her? This was not the way I wanted to see in the new year, but at least I could salvage this one part of it for her.

"Do you want to see the fireworks?"

She shook her head, reaching out to touch the bruise on my face with her fingertips, then slid her arm around the back of my head. I let her pull me closer to her, hearing her softly murmured words against my mouth, right before I claimed her lips. "No. I just want to be with you."

A couple of hours later, the room was full. My brother, Cass, Z, and Kinslee—all hanging around and getting in the way of me being with my girl. I didn't mind them being there, but I could see Winter was tired and fucking drained. She was still on the bed, propped up against the headboard, talking to Kins in a low voice, every now and then looking over at me like she wanted to make sure I was still there. Yeah, I wasn't going anywhere.

Z was on edge, restless, pacing the room, acting like he did after he'd done some shit that was fucked up—I never asked, but he had a lot going on. I'd done some fucked-up shit in my time, but Z? Some things were best left unasked and unsaid. I trusted him more than anyone, though. Even my brother.

"You okay, though? Really?" Cass dropped his heavy weight on the bed, staring at my girl with concern and running a hand through his hair. I never said it, but his relationship with Winter...fuck...I knew they were close friends, and I knew neither of them would fuck with their relationship with me, but I couldn't help feeling like if I wasn't around, he'd be all over her. It was most likely my fault, or karma or some shit, for taunting Winter with those other girls before we were together, but that image of her grinding on Cassius, him kissing her like he was fucking starving for her... Jessa had been forgotten the second I saw them together, and all my mind had thought was that Winter was mine.

Mine. No one else's. I'd hated her but wanted her at the same time—couldn't get her out of my fucking head. When I'd given in and had my dick inside her, feeling her coming around me, calling out my name, something shifted between us.

We were inevitable. And no one was taking her away from me.

"Cass." The jealousy sparked from an ember into an inferno, blazing to life. Why was I like this? He was one of my best mates, and she'd made it clear she only wanted me.

"Shit—uh, right. Boys, Kins. Let's go," he commanded, after doing a double take at my face. His expression would've been funny at any other time, but right now, I couldn't see any humour. Blame tonight. Blame fucking Hyde. Blame me. Whatever it was, I needed to be with my girl, with no one else around.

The room emptied out.

Then it was just us.

Winter was so exhausted that there was no way I'd add to all the shit she'd been through, but I climbed up on the bed, tugging her into my arms. She curled into me, her body small against mine.

"Thanks," came the soft voice from where her face was buried in my chest.

"Anything for you."

28

winter

"This is for your birthday. You can open it now or save it for the day." Arlo shuffled in his desk drawer for a minute, then handed me a small gift-wrapped package, and I stared at him, surprised and pleased.

"Thank you." I gave him a tentative smile. "I'll save it for the day, I think. Especially since we just got our Christmas gifts. Thanks again for mine, by the way."

Arlo had given me, Caiden, and Weston the exact same gift—equal amounts of shares in some tech start-up he'd invested in, and I'd been honestly shocked. And touched, actually. I hadn't been expecting to be treated the same as his own sons, and from the matching look of shock on my mother's face, neither had she.

He waved my thanks away, then indicated towards the door. "Just a token. Now, go and enjoy yourself."

With another smile I left his office, taking a detour to put the gift with the others in the bag waiting by the front door ready to take back home, then rejoined everyone else in the conservatory, or orangery, as my mother insisted on calling it. Whatever. It was glass and full of Arlo's bloody plants that seemed to love tickling me wherever I walked. My mother was having a small gathering since she and Arlo had been away for New Year's Eve, so consequently I and the rest of the Four were in attendance. Lena had managed to get out of it, but other than that, all the founding families were here, plus a select group of her and Arlo's closest friends.

"We must go shopping to find you some more appropriate clothing. Maybe I'll see if we can go with Arlo on his next business trip to London, if it doesn't interfere with your studies." My mother raked her gaze over me with a frown, pursing her lips.

I stared down at myself. What was wrong with what I was wearing? I knew how particular she was with clothing, so I'd worn a black, knee-length dress with an A-line skirt and heels. Demure, classy, and totally not an outfit I would have chosen for myself, but I was still working on the whole "keep her happy, don't make her suspicious" thing.

She must've noticed my confusion, because she added, "Your outfit is acceptable. I'm more concerned with your day-to-day attire. Jeans and hoodies are so uncouth."

Seriously? I rolled my eyes internally, and then a thought struck me. How was this even featuring on her radar? Every time I was in her presence I tried to dress as smartly as I could, unlike Cade, who still gave zero fucks. She was never around me when I was dressed down in my normal clothes. So how and when would she have seen me?

Making a mental note to mention this to Caiden, I just nodded, rather than replying. In return, she gave me a brittle smile that didn't reach her eyes, then excused herself to speak to Cassius' mother.

Making my way over to Weston, I dropped into the chair

next to him, accepting the glass of wine Allan handed to me. We both sat in silence for the most part, lost in our own thoughts. There was a weird, unsettled feeling in the air, which had been there ever since New Year's Eve. It seemed like everyone was on edge, waiting for the other shoe to drop.

We were all wary of Joseph, unsure of his game plan—but he seemed to have stayed quiet for the most part. Weston was constantly tracking my mother's and Arlo's cars. Frustratingly, there was still nothing out of the ordinary, not that they'd been back long from their ski trip.

What I couldn't work out was how everything was connected. It couldn't be a coincidence, could it? I couldn't help feeling I was missing an essential piece of the puzzle.

Sitting upright, unable to relax, I slowly sipped my wine, grimacing at the taste.

Weston glanced over at me with a short laugh. "Not a fan of wine?"

"Not really." I swirled the liquid around in the crystal glass. "Not of this particular wine, anyway—it's giving me a headache. I'll drink it to be polite, but I'd rather have Prosecco or champagne, if anything."

He craned his neck to look over at the tray with the bottles Allan had poured my wine from. "Just an FYI—that wine's something like five hundred quid a bottle."

"What?" I screeched, then instantly lowered my voice when several heads turned to look at me. "That's insane! I could buy, I dunno, a laptop or something for that."

He just shook his head at me, laughing, as I stared at him with my mouth hanging open.

"Something funny?" We both looked up, and Caiden was standing there, the corners of his mouth tipped up in amusement, his brows raised.

"Nah, just shocking your girlfriend with the cost of the wine she's drinking." West smirked at him, and his amused smile turned into a full-on grin, teeth and everything.

"My girlfriend," he repeated slowly, his grin widening. "Think you've had enough shocks for one week, haven't you, Snowflake?"

"Um, yeah," I mumbled, my mouth suddenly dry with the look he was now giving me.

"Both of you, come with me." His head cocked, he stared down at me, the grin still on his face, and without another thought I was on my feet, dragging Weston up with me, and we were following him out of the room.

He led us down the corridor to the small study we'd normally end up in and turned to West. "Do me a favour, will ya, bro? Go and hang out somewhere the others won't see you for a bit, so it looks like we're all together."

Weston huffed. "Fine, if I must. How long do you need?"

Caiden's gaze raked over me, the heat in his eyes lighting the fire within me that burned only for him. "We'll have to be quick. I'll text you when we're done."

"Alright. But you owe me, don't forget that."

"Yeah, yeah. When you get a girlfriend of your own, I'll repay the favour." Cade waved him off.

"Doubtful that I'll be getting a girlfriend anytime soon, but you still owe me." He slipped out of the room, and Cade locked the door behind him.

"Now, where were we?" He grabbed my hand and tugged me over to the polished sideboard under the window. "Right...stay there."

I stared at him, confused, as he crossed to the sofa and sat back, all casual and sexy, his legs kicked out in front of him. "What are we doing?"

His voice lowered to a rasp that went straight through me. “We’re doing our first kiss again. But this time, we’re going to continue doing what we should have done the first time, but I was too fucking blind to see what was right in front of me.” His tongue darted out to lick his lips, and his lashes lowered as he curled his finger, beckoning me towards him.

Fuck me.

“Um...pretty sure you weren’t the only blind one back then,” I stuttered, rooted in place.

“Yeah, so this is our do-over. Now, come here, Snowflake.”

“Are we doing it exactly the same way as before? Because I was really angry then. I can try and act angry—”

“As long as it starts with your mouth on mine and ends with you riding my dick, I don’t give a fuck. Now get over here.”

His words were the trigger I needed, and I practically leapt on him, fusing our mouths together, our kisses heady and biting, my arms wrapping around his neck as he gripped my hips, groaning into my mouth as I rolled my body against his.

He pushed my skirt up so it was bunched around my waist, and I ground myself against him, my underwear soaked. His heart was racing just as fast as mine as we devoured each other, hungry and desperate. “I need you inside me, now,” I moaned, panting, tugging on his hair as he left bites down my neck, his hand moving between us to unzip his trousers, shifting me on him so his cock could spring free. Fumbling in his pocket, he grabbed a condom, rolling it on, then roughly shoved my underwear aside. I moaned as my pussy slid over his hardness, coating his cock in my arousal.

"I'm fucking addicted to you," he husked against my mouth, as he lifted my hips, then impaled me on him.

"Cade," I gasped as he filled me completely, working his fingers over my clit, thrusting up as I rode him towards an orgasm that left me shaking and breathless.

"Fuck, I'm gonna come," he groaned, his head falling back. His dick jerked inside me as he came, emptying himself into the condom, and I leaned forwards, placing a kiss on his jaw as he muttered "fuuuuuck" on a long exhale.

He held me to him, both our breathing ragged as we recovered. He cupped my face in his hands, kissing me softly, before drawing back to look at me with a grin. "Better than the first time?"

I couldn't help smiling at the self-satisfied expression on his face. "I think you already know the answer to that question."

"I'm never gonna get enough of you, you know that, right? You're my fucking addiction, baby." He repeated his earlier words, all low and husky in my ear, and butterflies took off inside me.

"Same," I said, managing to get that one word out around the lump in my throat. Gripping the back of his head, I pulled him into a kiss, pouring everything I had into it, letting it show him how I felt, too scared to say the words aloud.

"I reckon we can get out of here," Cassius murmured to our small group in a low voice. I was standing in the corner of the orangery, constantly shuffling around since a particularly annoying tall plant kept tickling my ear, no matter where I stood. The rest of the Four were with me, minus Cade, who was talking to Arlo.

"Yeah, me too. We've been here long enough," Weston agreed, and Cass glanced over at Caiden and caught his eye. An unspoken communication passed between them, before Cade gave a tiny nod. He said something to his dad, and they shook hands, before he sauntered over to us.

"Let's go."

Finally. I swiped my tiny bag from the floor and slung it across my body. We started moving towards the door, before I paused, placing my hand on Cade's arm. "Hang on, I'd better go and say goodbye to my mother. You know she'll complain if I don't." He pulled a face, and I added, "You don't have to come. I'll meet you at the car."

He nodded, pretending to wipe his brow in relief, and I rolled my eyes. We split up in the hallway, the boys heading out of the front door while I made a beeline for the small sitting room where I was betting my mother was entertaining Cassius' mother and her other friends.

Entering the room, I looked around, but no sign of Christine. Estella was there, perched on the edge of a small chaise longue, gesturing in the air as she chatted to another woman. She noticed me hovering in the doorway and paused in her conversation to greet me.

"Evening, Winter. Are you looking for your mother?"

I nodded. "Yes. I'm just leaving, so I wanted to say goodbye on my way out."

She smiled, pointing to a row of glasses that stood on the low console table next to her chair. "I believe you'll find her in the kitchen, on the hunt for olives. We're having dirty martinis and we've run out."

"Oh no, that won't do," I found myself saying, internally shaking my head, and the corner of her lips tipped up in amusement as she clearly picked up on the unintended sarcasm in my voice. Oh fuck. This was awkward. "Thank you. I'll try there."

With a small wave, I backed out of the room as quickly as I could, my cheeks burning, and headed down to the kitchen, passing a huge, ornate gilt-framed portrait of my mother and Arlo, painted in oils, that hung on the wall, dominating the space. That was new.

I reached the kitchen.

I stopped dead, pressing my body flat against the wall, my heart beating wildly.

My mind tried to make sense of what I was hearing and seeing.

I didn't understand.

What the *fuck* was going on?

29

winter

The back of a head, a small bald patch in his greying hair, a phone pressed to his ear. Speaking in low, rapid-fire Russian (*I think*). One word flew out at me, as loud as if he'd shouted it.

Ivanov.

He turned, and I could see his profile, even though I knew who it was without a shadow of a doubt, the moment I saw his back, clad in the same classic black butler's outfit he wore constantly.

Allan.

I remained rooted to the spot, in total shock.

Allan finished up his call, then switched to speaking in English, his attention going to someone I couldn't see.

"They'll be in touch with details." His voice softened, as he took a step closer to whoever he was speaking to, and I carefully inched forwards, trying to get close enough so I could peer around the corner but still remain undetected. I could feel my heart pounding, and my palms were damp with sweat. "No need to worry. There's no sign that anyone suspects anything, and Hyde has already assured us that he will keep up his end of the bargain, in return for his promised share."

"I know. I suppose I feel a little apprehensive, what with the end finally in sight. One wrong move, and all my years of careful planning could come to nothing."

That was a voice I knew all too well.

My mother's.

Despite everything, though, until that moment, yeah, I knew she was involved in all this, but until I heard her voice, it hadn't really sunk in, I guess. The only way I could describe it was...you know when someone tells you something, but it takes seeing it for yourself to really hit home?

I hadn't realised how fucking much it would hurt.

Leaning forwards, I saw something that made my jaw literally drop, the way you read about happening but never think it happens to anyone in real life. Well, it happened to me. Right then. Allan was standing very close to her, his hand on her arm, squeezing it in a soothing, almost fatherly gesture, and she leaned into him, looking up at him with a... maybe not a *loving* expression, but the closest I'd seen to any kind of softness in her face.

He looked down at her, then turned his face away, barking out a cough into the crook of his elbow. "My apologies." He cleared his throat. "All will be well."

She straightened up, the expression disappearing. "I'm going back to the party. Could you serve another round of drinks to the men?" Then she opened the fridge, muttering, "Where are those blasted olives?" And without wasting another second, I slipped my feet from my high heels, swiped the heels from the floor, and fucking *ran*.

I reached the stairwell and skidded into the hollow under the curving staircase, placing my hand against the wall, trying to catch my breath. A minute or two later, my mother tottered past with a jar of olives in hand, followed not long after by Allan carrying a silver tray with various bottles and glasses balanced on top.

A sense of determination filled me. It was clear to me now that my mother and Allan both had secrets they were hiding, and I was *not* leaving here without any answers. I darted for the stairs—now was my chance, while I knew for a fact that Allan and my mother were both occupied downstairs.

Once at the top, I paused for a moment on the landing to shoot a quick text to Caiden. I needed a few minutes to check out Allan's room, and the last thing I wanted was for the Four to come barging back in the house, rousing suspicion. I knew they'd shout at me afterwards, but realistically, what was going to happen? Everyone else was downstairs, and I was going to be in and out as quickly as possible.

Me: Be a few more mins. Sorry. Warm the car up for me, it's a cold night!

It buzzed almost instantly with a reply.

Caiden: OK. I can think of a few ways to warm you up...

Yeah, I bet he could. But as much as I'd like to think about that, I needed to hurry up and check Allan's room. Which way was it? I tried to picture the layout of the house, and taking a guess that it would be at the opposite end of the house to my mother and Arlo's bedroom, I headed for the end of the long corridor, peering into rooms as I passed.

Nothing.

I reached the last door. This had to be the one. I just had to hope it wasn't locked. Closing my eyes and reaching out for the handle, I pushed.

The door slid open smoothly, and I breathed a sigh of relief. Slipping into the room, I carefully closed the door behind me, then took a moment to catch my bearings.

The room was large, as all the rooms were in this mansion, but much more simply furnished, the walls a plain, creamy colour with no ornamentation. Heavy, navy blue velvet curtains covered the windows, currently open and letting the view of the moonlight reflecting on the sea in through the window. Light was provided by a floor lamp standing in the corner of the room, bathing everything in a soft yellow glow. A large, mahogany bed with a navy bedspread stood at one end of the room, with a small table next to it. A dresser, again in the same mahogany, stood against the opposite wall, with a large wardrobe next to it. On the nearside wall was a bookcase, filled to overflowing with books, trinkets, and papers. A trouser press stood against the foot of the bed, and a large Persian rug covered the floor under my feet. I noticed a door, slightly ajar, which I assumed led into the bathroom as it was in the same position as the door in the bedroom that had been allocated for me here.

Where should I start? The bookcase was probably a good bet. I riffled through the papers—nothing of interest, mostly old clippings of various sporting events. It looked like Allan was a big football fan, as he'd saved articles on the Premier League going back years. Scanning the books, I noted that he was a fan of the classics—*The Count of Monte Cristo*, *Don Quixote*, and *War and Peace* were all among the hardcover editions weighing down the shelves. I guess I'd been hoping for something obvious, like maybe a book in Russian, or a Russian dictionary. Something to explain how on earth Arlo's very English butler could speak fluent Russian.

Of course, nothing could be that simple. No conveniently placed clues for me to find.

Where else could I look?

I got down on my hands and knees, checking under the bed, but the only thing I got was a face full of dust. Coughing, I clambered to my feet, casting my gaze around.

Only a few more places I could check in this room.

Crossing to the dresser, I eased open the bottom drawer, figuring if anything was likely to be hidden in here, the bottom drawer was the best bet. I carefully moved aside a scratchy woollen blanket, and my fingertips touched something solid.

Reaching forward, my hand closed around the item, and I lifted it out of the drawer. It was a solid wooden box, slightly smaller than a standard shoebox, with a hinged lid, with intricate carvings running over the lid and around the sides. I quickly pulled my phone out of my bag and snapped photos of the box at all angles, then sat down on the floor, cross-legged, to examine the inside.

I gently opened the tarnished gold clasp and lifted the lid.

It was full of letters, most yellowed with age, the ink faded and illegible.

Lifting the pile of letters out, I was about to unfold the first one, when I saw a glint of metal out of the corner of my eye.

My stomach churned as I touched the smooth gold sovereign-style ring, picking it up, already knowing what was going to be on it before I'd seen.

The cloaked man with arms outstretched, one holding what looked like a lightning rod, and the other resting on top of what was either a number eight or an infinity symbol.

The Strelichevo syndicate crest.

My heart was pretty much beating out of my chest at this point, and all I wanted to do was get away from this house, to escape to the safety of my boys, but I had to at least check these letters. I quickly snapped a couple of photos of the ring and let it fall back into the box, then returned my attention to the letters.

I unfolded the first with shaking hands, the paper crinkling under my fingers.

Then the next. Then the next.

All were in Russian.

I photographed the letters I'd unfolded, anyway, even though the ink was barely legible. There were no envelopes, so I didn't have a return address to give me any clue. Deciding to look at just one more, conscious that I'd already been here much longer than I'd planned, I opened the next one on the pile, and a photograph fell out, face down.

Lifting the photo from the floor, I turned it over in my hands and gasped aloud. The little girl in the photo looked so much like me when I'd been a child, that I instantly knew who it was.

My mother. Maybe around four or five, if I had to guess. What the fuck was Allan doing with my mother's photo and a box of Russian letters? I snapped another photo, then quickly piled everything back into the box and replaced it back in the drawer.

I'd just reached the door, when footsteps sounded in the hallway, and a barking cough that I recognised, since I'd only heard it ten minutes earlier.

Allan.

Fuck. Fuck. Fuck.

This was the last room in the corridor, which meant he must be headed straight for me. That, and the fact it was his bedroom. Where could I go? The bed was too low to squeeze my whole body under.

I was in full-on panic mode by this point, and I darted for the ensuite door, pulling it almost all the way closed behind me, just leaving a tiny crack that I could look through.

My panicked gaze darted around the darkened bathroom, my breaths shallow, a wave of dizziness assaulting me as I took in the tiny space.

Fuck.

There was nowhere to go. The bathroom consisted of a toilet, sink, and a white porcelain roll-top claw-footed bath with a shower attachment on the taps. Nothing else. Nothing to hide behind.

I was trapped.

All I could do was watch, with a dawning sense of horror, as the handle turned, and the bedroom door began to open.

30

winter

The window. That was my only option. Okay, I probably (definitely) wasn't thinking straight, but I couldn't exactly jump out in front of Allan, waving my hands like I'd appeared after some bloody magic trick.

Quickly, quietly, I made my way to the sash window, original to the house, which meant wooden frames and single panes of glass. I undid the catch that held it closed, and holding my breath, slid it upwards as carefully as I could. Luck must've been on my side, because it moved upwards smoothly and noiselessly. I guess I shouldn't have been surprised—knowing what I did of my mother, she probably had someone check all the windows on a regular basis to make sure they didn't creak.

Back in the bedroom, I heard a soft click as Allan closed the door behind him. I hoped and prayed with everything I had that he wouldn't come into the bathroom. I eased the window the rest of the way up, enough to create a gap I could slide through.

I threw my shoes through the opening, aiming for the manicured bushes down below, then without bothering to give myself time to think through this insane idea, swung my body out, gripping tightly to the sill. I scrabbled for a moment, allowing my feet to find purchase on the top of the wooden trellis that ran around the outside of the house, ivy growing over it. My bare toes touched the rough wood through the ivy and I breathed a sigh of relief. The trellis was narrow, but it gave me extra support while I held on to the windowsill with my right hand, my arm thrown across the length of the sill to give me extra support. Holding on with everything I had, I used my left hand to carefully ease the window shut.

Just as my hand dropped back to the windowsill, the light suddenly flickered on in the bathroom, and a sense of sudden panic hit me like a cricket bat to the head.

I. Let. Go.

I was falling, and fall—

I hit the tall bushes, scrabbling for purchase as my body bounced off the rounded top of the topiary, cut and shaped in a curve. I grabbed a handful of the hedge, managing to somehow stop my momentum, and dropped my body to the floor.

The cool grass, already damp with dew, was the most welcome relief under my body. My senses were in overdrive, and my flight instinct kicked in, telling me to get as far away as I possibly could, but if there was even a chance Allan was looking out of the window, he'd see me.

I waited.

A weird, vibrating sensation came from under my rib, and I shifted, pulling my tiny bag away from my body. I carefully drew out my phone, shielding it with my body, hiding the glow of the screen in case anyone was looking.

Caiden: Where the fuck are you? I'm coming back.

Shit.

Me: I'm outside. Round the back of the house.
Caiden: WTF?
Me: Be there in a few. DON'T COME FOR ME.
Caiden: Fuck that. Coming now.

Argh! He was so bloody frustrating, sometimes. Time to get out of here, and I just had to hope and pray that Allan didn't see me. Or anyone, for that matter. If Arlo's security caught me sneaking around the back of the house, I'd have some serious explaining to do.

Taking a deep breath, I crept around the side of the house, then ran for the gates, no thought in my head other than to get to the Four and get out of there.

"Winter!"

The shout came as I barrelled across the grass, running blindly in my bare feet, my heels left behind somewhere in the bushes.

Strong arms grabbed me from behind, pulling me back against a large body, and we skidded along the ground, losing our balance on the slippery turf. Then we were falling, and I landed with a thud, my face mashed into the cold, wet grass, unable to speak as the air had been knocked from my lungs.

Spots danced in front of my eyes as I struggled to take a breath, badly winded.

"*Fuck*. I didn't mean to hurt her!"

I could've sworn that was Zayde's voice.

"Let me get to her!"

Zayde's weight was suddenly gone, and I could breathe again. I lay there, kind of stunned, and then I was suddenly lifted, surrounded on every side by pure, hard male.

Muscles. Fucking delicious ocean scent. Strength but gentleness. Arms holding me tightly.

I burrowed into his warm body, sliding my arms around him. He carefully carried me, lifting me into the car, then pulling me back to him. He tightened his grip on me, running his fingers through my hair, and I closed my eyes.

I felt the rumble of an engine, and we were on the move. He held me still, cradling me in his arms.

"It's okay, baby. I've got you."

I was starting to feel a little awkward. Now we were safely back at home, Caiden had deposited me on the sofa and was currently pacing up and down in front of me, his jaw set. The others were giving each other sidewards glances, which I translated as "you be the first to speak." "No, you do it."

Finally, Weston broke the silence with a heavy sigh. "What happened to your shoes?"

I chewed my lip. They weren't going to like this. "Um... they're in the hedge somewhere around the back of your dad's house."

"What the fuck were you doing?" Cade stared at me accusingly. "You'd better not have gone off on your own again."

"It was a total accident. I didn't mean to...I overheard something." Before he could say anything else, I held up my hand. "Just a minute. Answer me this—how long has Allan worked for your dad, and how well do you know him?"

"Allan? What's Allan got to do with anything?" Weston stared at me, confused.

"About nine years. We know him well enough." Caiden

stopped pacing and spoke slowly, the same confusion entering his gaze.

"What about his family connections, friends, things like that?" I looked between Caiden and Weston.

"Winter? What's this all about?" Weston leaned forwards in his seat, his whole body tensing up as he took in my seriousness.

I swallowed hard, glancing up at Caiden. "You might want to sit down for this." He frowned but sank down next to me on the sofa, and I reached out to grip his hand. "Something happened."

I told them the whole story.

The four of them sat in stunned silence, but as I described how I'd decided to check out Allan's room, the air grew thick with tension. Caiden's eyes darkened, and he let go of my hand, clenching his fists, and the others eyed me with varying expressions of disapproval. When I got to the final part, where I heard Allan coming and escaped out of the window, Caiden went very, very still. As soon as I stopped speaking, he stood without another word and stormed out of the room, slamming the door behind him.

Shit. "He's really angry with me, isn't he?" I asked the room in general.

"You were irresponsible and you put yourself in danger. Fuck, Winter, couldn't you have even given him a heads-up?" Cassius shook his head at me. "Do you know what he was like when you were missing? He was out of his mind with worry. He's afraid of anything happening to you—we all are, for that matter. You're his world, and for you to go and put yourself in danger like that, without telling any of us... And on top of that, he finds out that Allan is most likely a bad guy..." He trailed off with a shrug. "Y'know?"

"I thought I'd be okay." My voice was small. "I'm

really sorry, guys. I honestly thought it would be a quick in-and-out kind of thing while he was downstairs."

"The window, though? You could've slipped and broken your back!" Weston glared at me, the anger in his eyes mixed with worry as we stared at one another.

"I'm really sorry," I repeated. The guilt swamped me as I took in their faces.

"I'm gonna go and investigate Allan. Just be careful, please?" Weston stood and crossed over to me, leaning down to kiss the top of my head, before stalking out of the room.

I needed to see Caiden. Standing, I went to follow Weston out of the room, then stopped in the doorway at the sound of Zayde's warning. He spoke low and evenly, but his tone was coated in ice.

"He's *not* happy. Don't antagonise him any further."

Without looking back at him, I nodded once, then slipped out of the room.

Heading towards the stairs, I paused in the hallway as I noticed the door to the basement was ajar. Acting on instinct, I switched directions and pulled the door all the way open.

The sound of the punchbag being hit drifted up towards me, and I tiptoed down the stairs, to be treated with a sight that took my breath away.

Caiden, bare-chested, his torso glistening with sweat, going at the punchbag with everything he had, absolute fucking fury on his face. The bag was swinging madly as he punched it over and over, his knuckles red and split—fuck, was that blood?

Why was I instantly wet?

I needed him. Right. Now.

"Caiden." My voice was hoarse, but I managed to speak loudly enough that his head snapped round to mine.

"*You*," he growled, and then he was stalking over to me, his eyes so, so black, a dark rage filling them. He reached me and thrust his hand up, gripping my throat, and pinned me against the wall.

I couldn't speak, not because he had his hand around my throat, but because I couldn't think enough to form words. I was on fire.

This was so fucked up.

He leaned closer, his teeth bared. "*You*," he repeated, then sank his teeth into my neck.

Flames of desire lit up my entire body, and I barely registered the pain.

I wasn't afraid. I trusted him with every single part of me—I knew he wouldn't go too far. All I knew was that I was beyond turned on, and the only thought in my mind was that I wanted him. The throbbing need between my legs grew more and more intense.

How to snap him out of this? I reached down and grabbed his other hand, pulling it up to my lips before he had a chance to react. His head flew up, and he stood, frozen for a moment, his eyes glued to my movements as I licked across his split knuckles, the burst of blood in my mouth coating my tongue with its sour, metallic tang.

It was a spur-of-the-moment, totally unplanned action, but…fuuuuck. It worked.

He lunged for me, attacking my mouth, ripping his hand away from mine and undoing his jeans with one hand. Not quick enough, apparently, because he suddenly released his grip on my throat and pulled away from me totally, pulling his jeans and boxers off, his cock hard, thick, and heavy between us.

My mouth watered. I needed him inside me, now, and we were most definitely on the same page. He tore my underwear away from my body before I could even process what was happening, and then he lifted me and thrust up into me.

"You. Were. So. Fucking. Careless," he hissed between thrusts, all teeth and savage grip on me. All I could do was hold on and ride him, moving closer and closer to the edge, feeling him flex around me. His hot breath on my face, his sweat-soaked body, his cock that filled me so perfectly...

"I'm sorry." My strangled gasp was barely discernible as he buried his face in my shoulder again, biting down, pressing me into the wall as he fucked me mercilessly.

Oh. Fuck.

Fuck.

Fuck.

Stars burst beneath my closed lids as I came hard and fast, gripping him with everything I had. His iron grip tightened on me as he followed me over the edge, pulsing inside me, his cum marking me as his.

"Caiden." I breathed his name as he kind of collapsed back onto the workout bench behind us, me straddling him, my arms around his neck, his dick still inside me.

"What am I gonna do with you?" His voice was so pained, and I knew what he was saying. Why had I been so stupid? He already had to go through losing his mother, and then to have me disappear not once, but twice, if you included tonight...*why* hadn't I at least sent him a message? What had possessed me to climb out of an upstairs window? Why didn't I think?

"I'm so fucking sorry, Cade. Please..." I had the biggest lump in my throat, and I could hardly get the words out around it. I swallowed, still breathing hard. "Please..." I took a deep breath. "Please don't do anything rash. I—I don't..."

Argh. My huff was audible—it wasn't meant to be.

"You don't what?" The rage and pain were masked by something else. Curiosity, perhaps?

I drew back to meet his eyes.

There he was.

My boyfriend.

His gaze all stormy, still angry, but tempered with his curiosity and what I thought was concern. And maybe something else, something I couldn't think, let alone say aloud.

He made my heart skip a beat.

"When you look at me like—" I stammered, flustered.

"Like what?" His voice grew impossibly soft, as he cupped my face in his hands, not allowing me any escape from his intense gaze.

"Like...I don't know. Like you care." I lowered my eyes, unable to look at him anymore.

He lifted my chin, forcing me to meet his gaze again.

"I do care. So fucking much. Why do you think I was so angry? You could've called or sent a message. We could've created a diversion for you so you could get out without putting yourself in danger!" His eyes closed for a moment, a muscle ticking in his jaw, before he turned the full force of his stormy gaze back on me again.

Being the centre of his focus?

It was like being in the hottest part of a fire.

He burned my defences away, leaving the truth exposed.

But I couldn't say it.

Couldn't think it.

I threw my walls up over the top, smothering the flames.

"I wasn't thinking."

"Remember what happened to my mum? Remember what happened to you, when you were fucking taken!"

His voice echoed around us, full of the pain he'd never shown me. Yeah, he'd told me about his mum, but this depth…the absolute despair in his voice…

The walls cracked and crumbled, burning away in an instant.

"I love you."

My words, shocking us both, hung in the air, then crashed to the ground.

Absolute silence.

Fuck.

"I—I didn't—"

"I fucking love you," he breathed against my lips, and then his mouth was on mine and we were kissing, pouring everything we wanted to say into this kiss. No other words were needed. Nothing else existed in that moment.

Just him and I.

31

winter

He loved me.

He. Loved. Me.

"I'm still angry, by the way." He finished dressing, glancing over at me where I sat on the weights bench, my legs still shaky. A small smile played across his lips as he registered the happiness that was probably beaming all over my face.

"I know. But you love me, right? So you can't be angry forever."

"You're fucking impossible," he growled, stalking over to me and pulling me up and into his arms. "Yeah. I do. I won't be angry forever, but don't push me right now, okay?"

"Say it," I begged, linking my arms around his neck. "I want to hear you say it."

"For fuck's sake," he muttered, before kissing the tip of my nose. His arms tightened around me, and then his eyes met mine. "You're mine, and I love you. You got under my fucking skin the first day I met you, and I never managed to escape."

"Did you want to escape?" I raised a brow at him, smirking.

He rolled his eyes. "You know I did. It was like you were sent here to purposely test me, to fuck with my head."

"Uh, same for me, thanks. You were fucking with my head just as much."

"That's true. Who would've thought you'd fall for your stepbrother, huh? What will our parents say?" He grinned at me, the anger in his gaze finally gone.

"I have no idea, but that's going to be one awkward conversation. Not that I care. I love you, Cade, and we'll get through whatever shit gets thrown at us."

"Yeah, we will. Come on, I'm gonna have a quick shower, then we need to sit down and find out what the fuck is going on with Allan."

He let go of me, and I dropped my hands from his neck, taking a step back. "I'll see you up there."

"No." Reaching out, he gripped my hand firmly and started tugging me towards the stairs.

"What?" I stared at him, confused, and he glanced over at me, giving me that wicked smirk that he knew I couldn't resist.

"Part two of your punishment for the way you acted. I need you in the shower to wash my dick."

Riiight.

"With your mouth," he added, his smirk widening into a huge grin.

"Oh, really?"

"Yep."

"Just how many parts to this punishment are there?" I asked curiously as we made our way up the stairs, excitement building inside me as I watched his eyes darken.

Dirty, dirty thoughts filled my head as he contemplated my question.

He licked his lips. "I'm thinking...at least five."

"I'm okay with that."

Back all together, minus Weston, who was busy digging for any data he could get his hands on, the mood turned deadly serious as the reality of what I'd discovered about Allan sank in.

"He's always been so quiet and unassuming. I never once would've imagined he'd be involved in any of this." Cassius rubbed his chin, deep in thought. "Nothing adds up."

Caiden nodded in agreement, his eyes on my phone as he scrolled through the photos I'd taken. "That's the fucking problem. Not even a hint of trouble."

"Except—" Zayde hesitated, and we all turned to look at him. The look in his eyes gave me chills. "I need to speak to Creed. I'll be back."

Caiden, Cassius, and I exchanged glances as he got up without another word, stalking out of the room.

"What was that all about?" Cassius wondered aloud. "Any ideas, mate?"

Caiden shrugged. "None. He's never said anything to me about Allan. Nothing suspicious, anyway."

"Is it worth speaking to your dad?" I leaned closer to Caiden, and he gave me a quick smile, tugging me closer and putting his arm around me.

"Yeah, I could. But I'd rather keep that as our last resort, if we can't find out anything else. I don't think my dad's involved, and I don't wanna make him suspicious."

"You didn't think Allan was involved though, either," Cassius pointed out.

Caiden stiffened next to me, and I frowned at Cassius. *Don't*, I mouthed, and he grimaced, his thoughts clearly turning in the same direction mine had. Enough shit had happened for one day. I didn't want Cade stressing about his dad on top of everything else, questioning everything he knew.

"Nah, your dad's not involved. I'm sure of it." Cassius blew out a heavy breath. "I'm not convinced that all this shit with Allan is as it seems, either."

We sat in silence for a moment, Cassius motioning for Caiden to pass him my phone so he could look through the photos.

"You okay?" I stared up at Caiden, worried.

"I don't know."

Sadness filled me at his despondent tone.

"Cade..." I slid my arms around him, and he held on to me tightly, as if he needed me to support him. As much as I needed answers, and as strong as he was, he'd been through so much in his life, and to now have all this to deal with... It was enough to shake even the strongest person. "We're going to get through this, okay?"

He didn't answer me, but he placed a soft kiss on my forehead, pulling me into him.

"Winter's right. We're so close to putting these puzzle pieces together. Failure is *not* an option. We're gonna get the answers, fuck some shit up, then get back to our lives." I looked around to see Cassius holding out his fist, his expression resolute.

Caiden released me, reluctantly I think, and they bumped fists, a smile finally back on my boyfriend's face.

"C'mon, babe. You have to do it, too." Cassius held his

fist out to me, and I was just about to respond when Weston crashed into the room, throwing a set of keys to Cassius.

"We need to go, right now. Cass, you're driving us to the docks. I'll explain on the way."

In the car, the second Cassius had started the engine, Weston continued, twisting in his seat to look at us, his leg bouncing restlessly, excitement in his eyes.

"Allan, nothing, total dead end, although I didn't have much time to look. But...call me a fucking genius. All the Alstone Holdings places other than AMC—the offices, warehouses, docks? Staff have an ID card they use to scan in and out with. I've been working on getting into their system for ages so I could match up the IDs to see if we could build up a picture of who was where and when. When I was searching for Allan, I had I guess what you could call an epiphany, and I managed to access the system. Finally! They had the strongest security I'd come across, as strong as Dad's." He paused in the middle of his speech, a thoughtful expression stealing across his face. "I wonder if it's the same as Dad's? If so, I might be able to hack his system at long last."

"Get to the point, will you?" Caiden stared at him impatiently.

"Yeah, sorry. I didn't dare to stay in the system for long in case I was detected, so I went straight to the date Winter was attacked, and the date she was rescued, on the off chance we might find an answer." Taking a deep breath, he met my eyes. "There's only one ID logged for the night you were attacked, which we have to assume was the guard. All the IDs are a long string of numbers, so I can't match them up to names yet. The night you were rescued? Same ID. But that wasn't the only one. Someone else was there, and the time they scanned in correlates with the rough time frame you were rescued, if we go by the time Kinslee got the phone call from the hospital."

"But how do we find out who—"

"Wait," he interrupted me. "I'm getting to that. That same ID has just scanned in at the docks. They literally did it as I was in the system, so they won't have been there long. There's one other ID already logged in, which I'm assuming will be the security guard, but that's it."

I gripped Caiden's hand tighter, my heart rate speeding up. Were we about to come face to face with my potential rescuer?

"Fuck!" Weston exclaimed, holding up his phone. "The answers are coming thick and fast. Not only are we about to find out who rescued Winter, or at least, find out who else was there at that time, but Mercury has info waiting for me. He says he's found out what Andromeda is."

What?

Hope soared in me. At last, we were going to get some answers.

We sped towards the docks, and Cassius threw his SUV into the layby I'd parked in way back when I'd first come here to investigate.

"Everyone stay together. Stay cautious," Caiden commanded in a low tone. "I've sent Z an SOS message, so he'll be here soon."

Moving stealthily towards the entrance, we fell into complete silence. Caiden kept hold of my hand the entire time but stayed in front of me, protecting me, while Cassius and Weston fell back in line behind me.

We could see the outline of the night guard in the hut, reclined in his chair, scrolling through his phone. It was easy enough to sneak past him and around to the long, low warehouse.

I sucked in a sharp breath, as all four of us stopped dead once we rounded the corner, staring at the figure that Caiden had almost run straight into.

My gaze travelled up, past the black boots, the jeans, the leather jacket, to the face, and our eyes met, mine widening in shock.

"*You*!"

TO BE CONTINUED...

ACKNOWLEDGMENTS

I'll *attempt* to keep this on the short and sweet side (doubt I will manage it). First of all, thank you for reading The Lies We Tell, and then choosing to read The Secrets We Hide. It means so much to me!

I have to once again thank my husband (not that you will read this), for helping me out with my research and reading the entire book, and only rolling your eyes a few times.

Thank you to Claudia and Jenny. You do so much for me, and I'm forever grateful. You both read the rough first draft of TSWH without complaining, and have been there for me through all my mental breakdowns, giving me support and encouragement when I need it most. Love you both, and I'm so glad I have you in my corner. Also - thank you Jenny for your amazing PA skills (and hot AF graphics), my life feels way less disorganised now!

Sue, Ashley, and Andi - thank you so much for taking the time to read TSWH through, and catch all the plot holes and errors I missed. I appreciate everything you do!

My amazing street team, you never fail to blow me away with all that you do. Thank you so much <3 And my ARC team, you are all amazing, and I thank you for taking the time to read and help get TSWH out into the world.

Sandra, my editor, and Jeanette, my cover designer, this book wouldn't shine without you. Thank you for all your hard work in shaping TSWH into the book it is now!

To the bloggers, bookstagrammers and readers that have shared, posted, commented, made edits, sent me kind words, joined my BBB group after reading... thank you for loving the Four. I'm so grateful for all that you do. While I can't promise 10 books for Cassius (haha), I can promise that each of the Four will get their own story.

Thank you for reading! <3

Becca xoxo

ALSO BY BECCA STEELE

LSU Series

Blindsided (M/M)

The Four Series

The Lies We Tell

The Secrets We Hide

The Havoc We Wreak

*A Cavendish Christmas (free short story)**

The Fight In Us

The Bonds We Break

Alstone High Standalones

Trick Me Twice

Cross the Line (M/M)

*In a Week (free short story)**

Savage Rivals (M/M)

Boneyard Kings Series (with C. Lymari)

Merciless Kings (RH)

Vicious Queen (RH)

Ruthless Kingdom (RH)

Other Standalones

*Mayhem (a Four series spinoff)**

*Heatwave (a summer short story)**

London Players Series

The Offer

London Suits Series

The Deal

The Truce

*The Wish (a festive short story)**

Box Sets

Caiden & Winter trilogy

**all free short stories and bonus scenes are available from https://authorbeccasteele.com*

***Key - M/M = Male/Male (gay) romance*

RH = Reverse Harem (one woman & 3+ men) romance

ABOUT THE AUTHOR

Becca Steele is a USA Today and Wall Street Journal bestselling romance author. She currently lives in the south of England with a whole horde of characters that reside inside her head.

When she's not writing, you can find her reading or watching Netflix, usually with a glass of wine in hand. Failing that, she'll be online hunting for memes, or wasting time making her 500th Spotify playlist.

Join Becca's Facebook reader group Becca's Book Bar, sign up to her mailing list, or find her via the following links:

facebook.com/authorbeccasteele
instagram.com/authorbeccasteele
bookbub.com/profile/becca-steele
goodreads.com/authorbeccasteele

Printed in Great Britain
by Amazon

39187448R00151